The Vegas Job

By
William Coleman

Copyright © 2019 by William Coleman

All rights reserved. No part of this publication may be reproduced or transmitted in any form or by any means, electronic or mechanical, including photocopy, recording, or any information storage and retrieval system, without permission in writing from the copyright owner.

This book is a work of fiction. Names, characters, places and incidents or either a product of the author's imagination or are used fictitiously. Any resemblance to actual people, living or dead, events or locales is entirely coincidental.

Cover Art by mojopad design © 2019

Nuremberg, Germany

ISBN 9781709121531

For Dominic
(AKA The Dude)

Also by William Coleman

Ponopolis - Book One
Into the Slaughter

ACKNOWLEDGMENTS

A very special thanks to Sheila Knowles for her editing and unique perspective. A big thanks to Karin Lauter (Giffy) for her patience, understanding, and support. And a shout out for anybody who took the time to read it – reviews appreciated.

\<pono\> from Greek: meaning pain.
\<polis\> from Greek: meaning city.

The Vegas Job
Part I

Saturday: Hour 54

"Hey man, you got a smoke?"

"Dude. No, I do not. I don't smoke and please don't ask me again." That was the fourth time he'd asked me for a cigarette. I'd leave, but someone else would just ask me for one; half the crowd in the place were suffering from nicotine withdrawal.

"I'm Jonesing for a smoke, man."

I picked up my book and leaned back on my bunk, the flat six-by-three concrete and steel slab which extended from the wall of the cell. *Yep*, I thought, *the B is in a fucking jail cell.* I opened my book and stared down at the pages. I wasn't reading it; I needed to think, and if you looked like you were reading a book, the other inmates left you alone—most inmates. Jamey, my wired-out little cellmate, never gave his mouth a rest.

It's been two days now since the Vegas job. Two days since I got arrested and thrown into the Clark County Detention Center, the Las Vegas jail, located downtown two blocks from Fremont Street—the old strip. I can see the back of the Golden Nugget Hotel from my small cell window.

They can only hold me for seventy-two hours without charging me for a crime. My story was as thin as pop-lyrics, but as hard as I tried, I couldn't think of anything they might have on me. They had less than one day to find something or cut me loose.

The first two days, they bunked me up with Larry, a short stocky African-American with long dreadlocks. In our time together, he asked me once for my name, and twice to please wake him before mealtime; he was truly a man of few words —unlike Jamey. I don't know what he did on the outside, but here, he used the time to catch up on his sleep. He could snooze away a good sixteen hours a day.

Late Friday evening a CO walked in and told Larry someone had posted his bail. He quietly stood up, stretched and yawned, before shuffling out the cell door. He didn't even say goodbye.

Less than three hours later, Jamey walked in, a CO in-step behind him, his arms extended stiffly to the front with his bedsheet, blanket and issued toiletries, neatly stacked, and carried oh-so-carefully. He was quiet the first night; everybody is quiet on their first night. But he hasn't shut up since waking up—I miss Larry.

"Man, I'm hungry. What time is lunch?" Jamey was standing at the cell door, bouncing up and down on the balls of his feet which were clad in bright orange socks and the orange rubber slippers that we all wore. Jamey was thin, and the baggy issued denim pants made him look ridiculously thin. Bobbing there, with his big orange feet, he looked like some kind of exotic Asian bird.

"We ate breakfast an hour ago." I kept my eyes glued to the unread page of the book.

Jamey walked back to the slab-bunk across from mine and sat down. There was a two-and-a-half-foot space between the bunks. "What are you in for?"

I looked up from the page, stared at him for several seconds, and said nothing.

"Hey. I'm not prying, just passing the time, getting a little stir-crazy in here."

"Dude!" I said, "You got here ten hours ago, you slept the first eight, had breakfast, and you've been jumping around the cell for an hour. You'd better pace yourself."

Jamey had dark curly hair, the front curls were a little too long, and he constantly swept them out of his eyes. "Yeah, you're right. This time it might be a while, they're saying I assaulted a police officer."

He scratched the top of his head with both hands. "The first day is always the worst, the walls close in on me, suck-me-silly." He laughed and walked the five feet to the cell door, looked down the hall, walked back to his slab and sat down again. "Assaulting a police officer? Look at me, man! I'm about one-twenty—naked. The two cops together were about four-fifty. What a fucking joke."

I was feeling stupid staring at the unread words in the book. I looked up at Jamey, but said nothing.

"I was at one of my old haunts, an off-strip bar, just hustling a few drinks for fun. I wasn't working, I stopped that shit a year ago. Got a legit job washing dishes at Denny's, the one down by the New York. The guy was buying me a few drinks, nothing illegal. The fucking manager must have recognized me, called the fucking cops. They show up. I tell them to fuck off, I'm having a few drinks with my friend here. One of them grabbed me by the back of the neck like I was a Catholic altar boy. I tried to bite him, his partner must have zapped me because that's the last thing I remember."

Two rough looking dudes, one black, one white, wandered up to our cell door and looked in. They looked like bikers, the white guy had long hair and a goatee, three dots tattooed under his left eye, they both had a lot of ink, a lot of it looked like it had been done on the inside.

Jamey stopped talking. I sat quietly holding my book. I looked up at them as indifferently as possible.

"Hey fellas," said the white guy.

"Yoo," I said, "What's up?"

"Either of you got a smoke?" he asked.

"Sorry dude. Don't smoke."

"I do," said Jamey, "but I haven't had one since landing here." He smiled up at them. "And I would truly show my appreciation to the one who turned me on to a pack." To seal the point, he gave them a boyish wink.

The white guy stared down at Jamey, grinned, and said, "Thanks anyway." they turned and drifted down the hallway.

Jamey turned his attention back to me, "I've been here twice before, not the worst jail for you to land in, believe me. I once spent a weekend in Men's Central in L.A.; that my friend is an experience you can live without. Here in the Vegas lockup, it's half tourists. Because you know," he shrugged "what happens in Vegas… could land you in here for a spell."

Friday: Hour 33

It was about an hour after lunch. Larry passed out on his bunk about five minutes after we got back to our cell. He was a quiet sleeper; the man didn't snore, you could barely hear him breathe. I was tired but too wired to sleep. The cops had questioned my story for over two hours. At around five in the morning they stuck me in this cell. I lay down on the hard bunk, not quite asleep, not quite awake.

A CO walked up to the cell door, "Nelson, you got a call."

I walked into a small hall, there were small payphones mounted on the wall placed about four-feet apart.

"Phone three," said the guard. He left and closed the door.

"Good morning, Billy."

"Morning Ray."

"Slept well?"

"Oh yeah, slept like the pussy in the parlor."

"Damn Billy, what did they pick you up for?"

Who knew if they were listening? Ray was trying to find out what story I'd told the cops; good if we're all on the same page.

"Wrong place, wrong time; I was looking for a party. They thought I was in on breaking into some building. I didn't break into shit. The door was open. I walked in, didn't see anyone, heard nothing;

thought I must be in the wrong place, I split."

"Did they charge you with anything?"

"No. Man, they haven't told me shit."

"Where did you hear about the party?"

"Do you remember the blonde I was talking to backstage after the show?"

"Yeah, I do. She was kinda cute."

"She told me there was a killer party going on, just north of downtown off the freeway. She told me how to find it, told me she had to meet her friend first and she'd hook up with me there."

Ray paused. I sensed he wasn't happy about that part of the story either. "Stick to the truth," said Ray, "It's a big mistake. We'll get you out of there."

Everybody but Ray calls me B, folks have been calling me B since I was sixteen. Why B: partly from my name, partly from my instrument, I play bass in a band called Road Dust.

Ray is the founder and bandleader. I joined the band six years ago. Road Dust has become more of a family than any band I've ever jammed with. We've been through it all, tours, studio recordings, good gigs, bad gigs, worse gigs, and jobs. Yeah, jobs, lots of jobs—thieves of the new millennium. We're still in it for the songs, but who the fuck buys CDs anymore. We'll drive into your town, entertain you, rip some shit off, and mosey on down the highway to the next gig—rock 'n' roll.

Saturday: Hour 59

At four o'clock they moved me to a holding cell two floors down. I still had the book in my hand, I picked it up in the dayroom where a lot of books were lying around. It was Kurt Vonnegut's, *Welcome to the Monkey House*, a book I had never read. I glazed over the blurb on the back cover. It seemed to be a collection of short stories. One day, when this is all behind me, I'm gonna read this thing.

I stared down at it. The front cover was a picture of a monkey behind bars—*funny!*

My thoughts drifted back to three days ago, when we'd arrived in Vegas. It was the highest paying job we'd ever taken. The payout was two hundred and fifty thousand dollars. Enough money to record our new LP and float the band financially for a while.

The brothers—AKA the twins—hired us to do the job. A lot of our work came down from the twins. I've never met them, Ray knew them from way back.

Las Vegas

We arrived in Vegas early Wednesday evening. We'd played the night before at the Silver Pony in Phoenix—always a lively crowd at the Pony. We'd booked a five-gig tour through the Southwest, all as an elaborate front for the Vegas job - but good clubs to play.

Ktel pulled our band RV, which we usually referred to as the Dread Sled, into the KOA campgrounds behind the Circus Circus hotel, though calling it a campground is a misnomer, it's a parking lot where RVs can park right off the strip, near all the Vegas action. Ray had reserved a site in the far corner right up on the fence. We'd have a little privacy, and we'd have our own private exit.

Ray jumped out of the camper and ran into the little office at the entrance, I sat at the table behind the driver's seat. Ktel sat behind the wheel scanning the small sea of RVs. The colors looked pastel in the dusty urban landscape, the ground was paved with asphalt with a few islands of dried worn-out grass.

I looked around the camper; it's a twenty-year-old Winnebago Warrior with a fading band logo painted across both sides. It isn't the prettiest thing on the road, but we call it home when we're on the road. Mal was sitting across the table lost in a book, something from Gloria Steinem—never heard of her. Mal, short for Malicia, is keys, fiddle and backing vocals, on the jobs she usually works lookout or decoy. Rip, our drummer, was crashed out in the back; he'd had a rough night back in Phoenix and had disappeared after the show. He turned up after breakfast looking like a pile of day-old roadkill. Ktel—mixer, roadie, master of all things technical and mechanical; he's invaluable on the jobs, there aren't many locks or security systems that could outsmart Ktel. Yeah, that's my family, that's Road Dust.

Sitting in the small holding cell, staring down into the Monkey's face on the book cover, I wondered where they were now.

Leaving Las Vegas

Thursday morning

The band left Vegas on Highway 11. After a few hours of restless sleep, they took a quick shower at the Circus Circus campground, threw their lawn chairs and a small grill into the storage well in the side of the RV and checked out.

Ray drove, Ktel sat shotgun, Mal and Rip sat across from each other at the small dining table. "We gotta get him out of there," Mal said, breaking the silence in the camper.

"Everything's cool," said Ray, keeping his eyes on the road. There was a lot of tourist traffic, probably headed to the Hoover Dam or Lake Mead. "I called the twins, they're gonna make some calls, there's a plan in the works. We decided not to call in any high-shooting lawyer yet, that'll just make the cops more suspicious. Billy's not a dumb-ass. He'll come up with some bullshit story why he was hanging around in front of a building that had just been robbed." Ray turned his head around, taking his eyes off the road and grinned at Mal.

"That ain't funny, man," she said. "B saved our asses last night."

"Relax Mal, we're gonna get Billy back."

"Well, why the hell are we leaving Vegas?" said Rip. "I feel like we're running out on him."

"We're not running out on anyone, just getting out of the city, lie low. The twins said it'd be safer, in case they come looking for the whole band," said Ray, while pulling the camper off Highway 11 and onto 93.

Ktel watched a golf course roll by, the lush greens contrasting with the dry brush and sand, "Who the fuck builds a golf course in the middle of the fucking desert."

Ray chuckled, "The guy that knows there are enough stupid assholes who'll fly out into the middle of the Mojave and pay a lot of money to walk around on it in a hundred-and-twenty degrees. That's who."

"Who'd want to talk to us?" asked Mal.

"Are you forgetting who we ripped off?" asked Ray. "Fabian, Fabian fucking Delbowski. We talked about this. The guy is no lightweight. He owns a string of small casinos in the Vegas metro area. He owns two titty bars, one of the biggest brothels, The Rooster Ranch, and real estate all over the Southwest; and that's just on paper, who knows what he's got going on under the table. I was straight up on that, the number one priority on this job was getting in and out clean. No one wanted us to steal a fucking one-of-a-kind guitar, probably the most famous guitar in the world to make money; you'd never be able to sell the fucking thing. This was politics. This was somebody sending a big fuck-you to Delbowski. Unfortunately, I don't have the whys, all I know is we were getting paid a lot of money to do a job."

Lake Mead jumped into view on the horizon, a big splash of blue in the middle of the sun-bleached browns. The highway curved to the south as they got closer to Hoover Dam.

Ray navigated back to the right lane, before continuing. "We're not worried about the cops. They got nothing on him, he was walking by some building when the alarm went off, one guy, alone, not a group of people wearing masks. He plays his story right, sits-tight, he'll be out by the weekend. The problem is Delbowski, somebody ballsy enough to break into his Vegas lair, steal his prized possession. He's gonna turn over every rock till he finds out who, and he's gonna want to talk with Billy."

"This is sounding really fucked," said Rip

"How are we gonna get him out?" asked Mal.

"We ain't gonna do nothing" said Ray. "We're getting out of the city. The twins are sending in their best team. I'm gonna call Billy in the morning, find out what line he used on the cops—just in case we need a lawyer."

The band drove down Highway 93, everyone lost

in their own thoughts. In the years of ripping shit off, they'd had some screw ups, but nothing this heavy. The job was going as perfectly as planned—until it wasn't.

The camper drove over the Colorado River and crossed the state line into Arizona. They could see the Hoover Dam standing majestically to the left, tourists crawling all over the top of it like ants.

Rip leaned forward and peered out the window at the big wall of concrete. "I heard there are bodies buried inside the concrete, workers that fell in and it was too expensive to get them out—just left them in there."

"That's a myth," said Ktel from the front seat. "If any workers fell into the concrete blocks, the engineers couldn't leave them in, the bodies would eventually decay leaving air pockets in the concrete. In the end, it would compromise the integrity of the dam."

"I'm just saying, that's what I heard." Rip spun around without standing up, opened the fridge behind him, and pulled out a can of 805 beer. "And, I've heard the story a few times."

"It's an urban legend." Ktel hopped out of his seat and sat down at the table next to Mal. "Grab me a beer too, man. I think the Hoover dam story comes out of another dam they were building in Montana around the same time. The Fort Peck Dam, it's an earth-filled dam, not concrete like the Hoover. There was a cave-in, eight workers were buried alive, they recovered only two of the bodies."

"Well, thank you for that history lesson professor Ktel." Rip grinned and handed Ktel a can of 805.

"You're welcome," said Ktel

Mal gave Ktel a friendly push. "Let me out."

Ktel stood and let Mal squeeze by, she hopped up and sat shotgun across from Ray. "Where the hell are we going, Ray?"

"Another mile or two, should be a turnoff coming up."

"We're deep in it this time, aren't we." Mal looking across at Ray.

"Yeah. We are. But I trust the twins, we go way back. We'll figure this thing out."

"This must be the turn coming up." Ray started slowing the RV down and turned right on a small two-lane road. The road wound back down toward the Colorado River, the dry landscape dotted with Barrel cactus, Cholla, and an occasional Joshua tree. After a mile or two they came to an old rusty ranch-style entrance gate. The name on the sign welded into the top of the entrance read: *Lloyd's Campground.*

Ray pulled in and parked in front of a run-down adobe house. It looked like it hadn't been painted in decades, there were large patches of wall that looked like they were crumbling apart. A small room extended out from the front, swoopy faded lettering on the window read: *Reception.*

Mal looked around the place. There was a big area in the center with about twenty small campsites for RVs. Every site was empty except for one corner site with a vintage Streamline trailer parked in it. Past that was a narrow brick set of stairs which led up to the top of a small hill—possibly a few tent sites. Mal couldn't imagine anyone wanting to sleep in a tent in this rattlesnake, scorpion-infested desert. On the north side of the grounds was a shower house and restrooms, also adobe, and in worse shape than the house. To the left was a gaping blue and green hole that looked like it had once been a small swimming pool. "What a dump. Where did you find this place?"

"Google," said Ray. "I found it online this morning before we left the Circus Circus. Looked like it'd be a quiet out-of-the-way place."

"It is that," said Mal.

Ray jumped up and walked out of the camper, "Let's see if anyone's around." He opened the door to the reception office and went in; a minute later he walked out, looked back at the camper and shrugged his shoulders. He walked around to the main house behind the reception and knocked on the door. After a minute he stepped back, held his hands up to his face and shouted, "HELLO." He stepped further around the house, there was a large tin garage shed behind in the back, almost half the size of the house. "HEELLLO!"

A small elderly lady with long bushy hair that had mostly gone to gray, stepped out of the shed. She was wearing baggy overalls, old brown unlaced work boots that looked too big for feet and she was covered from head to toe in a layer of dust. Her face looked like it was made of red porcelain from years of living in the desert "Hey there," she said in a western drawl. She stepped forward while removing her work gloves and tucking them under her left arm. She held out her right hand for Ray to shake. "The name is Polly, Polly Sosa. Pleased to meet ya."

Ray shook her hand, "Ray Loe. My pleasure."

She smiled, showing off big, amazingly white teeth for her age. "You lost, or are you looking for a place to park that Winnebago?"

"We're a country-rock band on tour, need a quiet place to take a break for a couple of days."

Polly turned her head and looked over the place, she made a puzzled expression, as if she hadn't realized until now how quiet and desolate the place was. "Well son, you've come to the right place. I take twenty-five a day for a site, and five a day per occupant."

"Sounds good," said Ray. "Which site should we pull her into?"

Polly turned and looked again at all the empty campsites. "Well, if you'll be needing electricity, best pull into three, four, twelve or sixteen. Them the sites with working electric. Oh wait," she said, holding her hand up, "The Babbitts got their Streamline in twelve. So, three, four, or sixteen would be your best bet."

"All right, I'll take one of those. Should I pay in advance?"

"Stop by the office later on. I'd like to get back to my repairs in the shed."

As Ray walked back to the RV, he wondered what repairs she could do in the shed that would be a higher priority than just about anything else in the entire dilapidated campground.

After circling around the campground's small outer ring, Ray pulled the Dread Sled into site three. They busied themselves setting up camp, Ktel plugging in the electrical hookup, even checked the amperage. Mal took one look at the greasy, sticky looking picnic table, "I'm gonna hit that table with some soap and water." She walked back into the camper muttering, "Maybe a few times."

Rip took one look at the site's grill pit, with its sooty broken grill lattice, and said, "I'll get our grill out and set it up."

After years of traveling around together in the Winnebago, they had their routine when it came to setting up camp. Everyone knew what had to be done, and just did it.

Later that evening, while Rip was getting some charcoals going on the grill and Mal was putting together a salad, a rusty old Ford pickup truck rolled into the campgrounds. It slowly drove by the Dread Sled, they could make out two faces peering out at them, but the windows on the truck were tinted and they weren't able to make out more than two shadows. Ray stiffened, but they weren't cops, and they didn't belong to Fabian Delbowski, the truck was more rust than truck.

The Ford pulled up next to the Streamline trailer and you could feel the tension ease.

Five minutes later, a couple ambled over to the Dread Sled, the woman was holding a plate covered with foil. "Hey there, neighbors," she said, the man shuffling along behind her. "My name's Sheryl, and this here's Rick." She was shortish, an upper welterweight sized early sixtyish woman wearing jeans, sandals, and a baggy tie-dye shirt. Rick was about five-foot-nine and looked like he did some running. He wore cargo shorts and a Bob Dylan Rolling Thunder Revue t-shirt.

Ray couldn't place the accents. It wasn't from down here in the Southwest, and it wasn't really Midwest either. "Evening ma'am. My name's Ray." Pointing everyone out using the neck of the beer bottle he was clutching on to, "This here's Ktel, Mal, and that's Rip over there trying to start a fire."

"I need some girl scout juice." Rip had torn up an old music magazine and was trying, unsuccessfully, to ignite the charcoal with it.

Sheryl turned to Rick. "Don't we still got a good supply of lighter fluid?"

"Yeah," Said Rick. "I reckon we do; I'll go and get one." Rick did an about-face and walked back to the Streamline.

"That'd be great," said Rip, tossing one last match into the grill, giving up on the torn-up magazine experiment.

"You're the first neighbors we've had in darn near a week," said Sheryl. "It was feeling kinda lonesome around here, 'bout never see Polly these days, got herself busy on some repairs. Can't be easy keeping the place up, now that Cesar's done passed. She's out in the mornings giving the bathrooms a once over, sometimes swings by in the evening to say hello. This place never gets busy this time of year."

"This place hasn't been half-full in years," said Rick, coming up behind Sheryl. He walked over and set a bottle of Kingsford lighter fluid on the picnic table.

"Much obliged," said Rip. "We may be low on fuel, but we got plenty of brats if you two neighbors wanna join us?"

Sheryl's eyes narrowed into a tight stare. Rip was wondering if he'd said something wrong. Sheryl burst into a hard deep laugh, "OH MY GOSH! I'm such an old dummy. I've been standing here the whole time, flapping my jaws, and I completely forgot about the brownies. Here you go," she handed the plate to Mal. "Maria was it?"

"Malicia, but most folks call me Mal."

"Road Dust. That's an interesting painting you got up on the side of your camper," said Rick, stepping over to inspect the mural.

"That's us," said Ray. "Road Dust. We're a country-rock band on tour. We just played Vegas, got a few days off before the next show."

Sheryl grinned and said. "I love country-rock. Where did you play in Vegas?"

"The Country Saloon," said Rip.

"That's down at the Fremont Street, isn't it," said Sheryl.

"We've been there," said Rick, "a few years back, I think." He held his chin while shaking his head. "Who was it we saw there?"

"Wasn't it the Avett Brothers," said Sheryl.

"Nah," Rick was shaking his head again. "We saw them at the open-air festival up in Reno. I think it was some local band, don't remember the name. It's a nice venue though, and the beer ain't priced too high, that I do remember."

"Where y'all from?" asked Sheryl.

"The band's from Ponopolis, Rip and myself are originally from Minnesota. Mal's from Chicago and Ktel is a native of Ponopolis. And you two campers, where are you from?" asked Ray.

"Piedmont. Piedmont South Dakota."

"That's in the Black Hills, beautiful country, I've been through there a few times. I played at the Sturgis Rally twice."

"Oh yeah. We're thirteen miles down the road from Sturgis," said Rick.

"My Ricky here. He was a fireman for the Piedmont Fire Department, he was the department's mechanic too, kept all the trucks up-and-running. I owned my little hair salon." Sheryl reached over, peeled back the foil on the plate that Mal had set down on the picnic table and took out a brownie. "I'm sorry, I haven't eaten since lunch and I'm starving." She took a bite from the brownie. "My daughter's running the place now, yep, The Valley Wash House Salon. I ran that place most of forty years."

"Anybody want a beer?" asked Ray. He walked over to the camper and stepped in. The incessant small talk was freaking him out. He needed quiet, he needed time to figure out how to get the band out of this mess. He had talked to Dan twice, they had a plan and if everything fell into place it could work. They had to get Fabian's focus off of Billy.

After dark, after everyone had had their fill of brats, store-bought potato salad, and an Asian salad that Mal had thrown together, they sat around the campfire sipping beer and listening to some tunes coming from the Dread Sled's sound system.

Ray hadn't heard more than five short lines from Rick all night, but Sheryl never really seemed to stop talking.

"I hope you got one more of those beers?" Polly walked up from around the backside of the camper. "Because I could really use one." She was actually a lot more petite than Ray had first thought, now that she wasn't wearing baggy overalls. She was cleaned up, her hair still wet from a shower, she wore jeans and a light blouse, white with large red roses.

Rip grabbed another chair from the well and folded it out for her.

"I'll get a few more beers," said Ray.

Everyone was talking, smiling, and laughing. Rick had told a joke, something about a truck on fire, but Ray couldn't get his mind off of Billy. He trusted Dan, but he hated sitting around, waiting, doing nothing.

The Vegas Job
Part II

The Country Saloon, located downtown on Fremont, booked us for Wednesday night. A good club to play, some locals, a lot of tourists, folks just drinking and looking for a good time. About three songs into the set we did our up-tempo rendition of *Ring of Fire* from Johnny Cash, that picked things up for the rest of the show.

Road Dust was headlining the show. The warm-up band was a local band called the West Coast Barnstormers. I was backstage chilling before the show and I didn't check them out, seemed like they were doing a lot of covers.

After the show, we hung out, had another beer with the Barnstormers, loaded up our equipment on the Dread Sled, and drove back to the campgrounds.

We waited, packed up a few things needed for the job, and waited for Mal to get into costume—she was playing decoy on this one.

Ray drew all the curtains just shy of two o'clock, left a few dim lights on, and turned on the TV at a low volume, in case some campers came snooping around.

Ktel threw an old rug over the chain-link fence and we all hopped over it—no one was hanging back on this one.

We walked along the fence, cut through the corner of the fairgrounds, stood on a small stone hump, and climbed over the wall onto Sammy Davis Jr. Drive. We walked across the street and down the block. There was a machine shop with a parking lot next to it. We had a burner car which Ray and Ktel had picked up earlier, a ten-year-old Impala, a common rental in Vegas.

We drove north on Fifteen, east on Five-Fifteen, and got off on North Eastern Avenue. The band was quiet, everyone lost in their own solitude, working out the kinks in their nerves. This was the biggest payout we'd ever had, we were on our way to rip off a Vegas boss, not one of the big bosses, but someone with serious muscle.

After a mile we turned left and came to a small warehouse district. We pulled into the lot of a large laundry service, Vegas has a lot of sheets to wash. A lot of people worked there, they ran three shifts, no one would notice a car coming or going. Right across the narrow parking lot divider was Maslo Corp, Fabian Delbowski's headquarters.

"This is it. Point of no return," said Ray from the front seat. "Everybody cool."

Ktel sucked in a handful of air through his nostrils. "I'm cool."

"Rip?"

Rip slapped a short drum roll out on his knee. "Cool."

"Billy?"

"Did you guys notice there's a big cemetery right across the street?"

"Billy."

"I'm cool."

"Mal, if you're on, you're up. You start this one."

Mal held up her hands, entwined her fingers, and gave her knuckles a good cracking. "I'm on it."

She stepped out of the car, walked across the divider and headed toward the front door of Maslo Corp. The building was a long rectangular box made of sheet-metal, the front section comprising two floors of offices. The larger, rear section of the building was a warehouse containing rows of old slot machines, casino tables, and a few old-timer cars. There was nothing of real value in the whole place, except the guitar, and that's what we were here for.

Fabian Delbowski and his crew were out of town, up in Reno for a meeting, and they'd be gone until Sunday. That's why this was the perfect night to hit the place. There was only one security guard stationed at the reception, a paid rent-a-cop, probably half asleep, and bored out of his mind.

Mal was getting closer to the door. "Let's roll," said Ray.

We had rehearsed this several times; the job wasn't complicated, but the timing was crucial.

Mal was dressed like an expired party-favor, crooked wig, smeared make-up, a sexy top which split open almost to the navel, a short black miniskirt, and pumps. She banged on the glass door with an open hand. "HEY THERE. HEEEY!" She banged again.

The security guard unlocked the door, opened it a few inches, and asked through the opening, "Yes, ma'am. How can I help you?"

Mal stepped forward, acted like she wanted to whisper something through the opening, tripped, fell forward through the door and flopped to the floor of the lobby. The security guard opened the door wider, spun around, and reached down to help her up.

I stepped up behind the guard grabbed him by the shoulder and pushed the end of a small steel pipe into the back of his neck—the pipe was about the same size as the barrel of a '38. "Freeze motherfucker! Or you will finish your shift with a big fucking hole in your neck."

The guard froze solid while his mind raced to catch up with his situation.

Rip came up beside me and stuck a small hypodermic needle into the back of his neck and pushed the plunger home. The guard instinctively reached up to his neck, but he was slow and Rip had already removed the needle.

"Fuck," he whispered before promptly passing out.

I eased him to the floor, spun him around, picked up his feet, started sliding him across the lobby and back behind the security desk.

"Damn," said Ray. "Worked even faster than on the poodle."

Ktel and Rip laughed.

A few weeks ago, Ray and Ktel reported that they had tested the drug on a poodle that belonged to Ktel's sister. I thought they were just yanking my leg—now, I wasn't sure.

Mal stood up and casually headed back to the car. She'd start the motor and wait for us.

We hurried up the lobby staircase, down the hall and stopped in front of a large double door. Ktel reached into his satchel and brought out a small electric screwdriver and a small claw-like tool. He kneeled down in front of the pin pad attached to the wall next to the door, quickly removed the two screws and used the claw to pop off the cover. He removed a similar-looking pin pad from his satchel and using four alligator clips attached them to three separate locations. A white LED light lit up on his pin pad. He punched in four numbers and the LED turned green and the door buzzed.

Ray opened the doors and swung them both wide open. "Hallelujah! There she is."

We all walked in. It was a large office, a good four-hundred square feet. A large oak desk centered on the back wall. The centerpiece of the room wasn't the desk; the centerpiece hung on the wall above the desk. A guitar hung upside down on a plush red plaque which was set in a gold-plated frame. The presentation was fantastic, we all stepped up closer to get a better look. The guitar was a stock '68 Strat with an Olympic white finish, an awesome guitar, but nothing to pay us yokels a quarter of a million to steal. No, the value was not in the guitar itself; the value was in the legend. This was Jimi Hendrix's guitar, this was the guitar that was slung upside down around his back at Woodstock, the guitar used to play his now-legendary rendition of The Star-Spangled Banner.

Ray and Rip walked around the desk and stood in front of the guitar. It was mounted on the plaque by eight red velvet-upholstered hooks, six on the body, three up, three down, and two hooks on the neck of the guitar. Ray reached up and slowly turned the three hooks that held down the top of the guitar. They both carefully lifted the guitar straight up from the bottom hooks. As soon as the guitar cleared the hooks, the one which secured the lower neck snapped down to the surface of the plaque making an audible click sound.

Ray and Rip froze. Ktel looked up at the wall. "Shit." less than a second later an alarm went off, echoing through the entire building. I could see several bright floodlights from the lobby flickering on and off.

Ray: "Bag!"

Ktel grabbed a rolled up guitar bag from his

satchel and slung it open across the desk. Rip slid the guitar in and we hauled ass out of the office and down the stairs. As we crossed the lobby, we could see cherry lights flashing from a block down the road.

"Fuck that was fast!" said Ray. "They must have been close."

As we approached the door, I could see two cop cars coming in fast, a couple hundred feet out. I knew we'd never make it; the time wasn't there. The cops would be on us before we got halfway to the car. I pulled my ski mask off. "Ray." He turned his head. I tossed him my ski mask. Our eyes caught, he knew what I was planning to do. He nodded.

We flew out the door. They turned left. I turned right, into the oncoming cop cars. I reached up and gave my eyes balls a good rub with my thumb and index finger, it stung, but it would help with the effect.

I wandered out in front of the bright oncoming headlights, waving my hands above my head. The two cars screeched to a halt with less than six feet to spare. I stood there, my hands still waving back and forth in the air. A spotlight hit my face, blinding me. "Hey man, I'm just looking for the party. She told me it was here." To help illustrate the idea I began pointing with my thumb back toward the building. Hands grabbed me and manhandled me to the ground. I felt the cold steel of the cuffs clasping over my wrists.

I lay on the ground, a cop still had his knee stuck in my lower back. "Man, this is not cool. It's me," I said, "B, I'm the bass player."

You Got That Love

Friday

In the morning, the band sat around drinking coffee, taking showers, and getting settled in. Mal was surprised that the coin-operated washing machine next to the showers actually worked. The dryer was ancient history; it looked like it hadn't worked in years—someone had taken it half apart and left its guts laying on the floor next to it. She got some rope from Ktel and tied it up between the camper and a lamppost to use as a clothesline. Rip whipped up some scrambled eggs, covered in a layer of sliced avocado, Monterey Jack cheese and chili peppers.

They were all sitting out on the picnic table drinking coffee after breakfast. "Good chow, Rip," said Ray.

"Thanks, man."

"Ain't seen the Babbitts all morning," said Ray.

"They took off early. I guess they like to play the slots all day while they're in Vegas," said Mal. She stood up and started piling up the breakfast plates.

"Mal, can you do me a favor," Ray said while topping off his coffee cup from an old tin percolator. "Could you run over to the office and pay off the campsite for three days?"

"Sure, let me get these first."

Ktel got up. "I'll give you a hand with them."

Mal wandered over to the office, it was empty, and like Ray, she walked around and knocked on the door to the main house—nothing. She heard a high-pitched pecking sound, at first, she thought it was coming from inside the house; she turned and decided it was coming from the shed. She walked over and turned the knob on the door; it was locked. She gave the door a good knock, "Polly!"

A half-minute later the door opened, Polly quickly popped out and closed the door behind, "Hi there," she said, smiling her big white smile. Like yesterday, she wore overalls, she was covered in dust, and sweating profusely.

Mal held up a few folded bills. "I came by to pay off our campsite."

"Well thank you," said Polly, wiping her brow with a red-checkered bandana. "I trust y'all ain't gonna skip out on me. I'll stop by and pick it up when I'm done with my work."

"Anything I can help with?" asked Mal.

She smiled even wider. "Why thank you, young

lady, it's hard to keep up the place now that Cesar's gone." She turned and looked at the shed, "But this is a repair I really need to do myself. You run along now, I'll be over shortly and pick up the money."

Polly hopped back into the shed and closed the door. A second later she heard the click of the lock. Mal stuffed the money back into her jeans pocket and walked back to the Dread Sled.

Saturday

Ktel's fingers deftly twisted the joint up in one quick roll, he slid his tongue across the edge of the paper, one more little twist, and then lit it up. The whole process took a few seconds. The joint was slightly thinner than a cigarette but looked like it had been machine rolled.

"Dude, after all these years, it's still fascinating to watch you roll a joint," said Rip.

Ktel took a deep hit, smiled, and passed the joint over to Rip. Mal sat next to him by the window reading a book. The three of them sat in the camper where it was cooler.

"With those fingers, why aren't you a lead guitar player, man? God knows Ray could use the help on guitar." Rip took his hit and gave Mal a nudge.

She looked up from her book. "Why not; this place already makes me feel like I'm in a David Lynch movie."

"Fuck," said Rip looking up. "Did we put nachos on the shopping list?"

"Yes," said Mal.

"Cool. In about ten minutes I'm gonna start getting the munchies. When do you think Ray will be back?"

"Fuck if I know." Mal was getting irritated, every time Rip spoke she'd lose her place in the book.

"He's been gone a while now."

"It's been about thirty minutes." Mal stuck the guitar pick, her makeshift bookmark, in the book and set it on the table.

Ray had driven into town with Polly to get some supplies. She was going into town anyway, and it meant they wouldn't have to disconnect the camper.

"Hope he doesn't forget to buy some pop," said Rip.

"What do you think she's doing in there?" asked Mal, looking out the window toward the house and shed.

"What who's doing where?" asked Rip.

"That old lady, Polly, in her shed. It's kinda weird. Every time I walk by the shed you can hear a pecking sound. She was secretive about it, couldn't even get a look inside."

"What do you mean, pecking?" asked Ktel.

"I don't know, like metal on metal."

"Maybe she's a blacksmith," said Rip.

Ktel took a hit off the joint and handed it off to Rip. "No chimney."

Before taking a pull off the joint, "Chimney?"

"If she was smithing in there, the shed would have a chimney," said Ktel.

Rip smiled, a penetrating smile, handed the joint off to Mal. "I love you, man."

"Let's go check it out," said Mal, her eyes beading down on the shed.

"Ain't none of our fucking business what that old lady's doing in there," said Rip.

"I'm a girl, I'm stoned, and I want to look in the shed. Ktel, I'm gonna need your skill-set for a minute."

"OK." Ktel stood up.

"Dude!" said Rip, throwing his palms up. "Are you serious? Ray will freak when he comes back. We're here to lie low."

"Chill out dude," said Mal. "We're only fucking around. Look around, it's just the three of us here. If you see anyone driving through the gate, text me, we'll have plenty of time to get out."

It took Ktel all of twenty seconds to get through the lock on the shed. It took their eyes a moment to adjust to the dim lighting in the shed. There were several small windows but garbage bags had been duct-taped over them. There was a long workbench running the length of the rear wall of the shed, tools scattered across the top, some hanging from pegboards. Piles of equipment were lying around the far end of the shed—shovels, rakes, hoes, boxes, bags, pretty much what you'd expect to see in a shed at a campground. Six feet down from the door was a large deep freezer, they could hear the rattle of the old compressor.

Mal walked over to the center of the room. "Well, now we know where the pecking sounds are coming from." There was an oblong indentation in the concrete floor where someone had been chipping away at it, a pickax was leaning against a support pole next to it to prove it. "Why would she want to take out the floor, the shed is the newest-looking thing in the entire campground?"

"No fucking clue," said Ktel "but she's going about it all wrong. It'll take a year for her to get through the floor with a pickax like that; best would be a jackhammer, or if you ain't got that, cover it with a sheet of plastic and break it up with a sledgehammer."

"Why tear up the floor, and why the big secret?" Mal walked over to the other side of the shed and looked at the piles of junk and well-worn tools, shook her head and walked back toward the door. She stopped and stared down at the damaged floor again and then stepped over to the freezer. She tried to lift the lid, but it was locked. She looked up at Ktel.

"On it," said Ktel. He pulled out his small satchel of picks, choose two, got down on one knee, and promptly jimmied the lock open. He stood up and lifted the lid.

Both Ktel and Mal took a quick step back. "Well,"

said Ktel. "Now the story is falling into place."

There was a lanky reddish-brown man haphazardly tossed into the freezer, and it looked like he'd been there a while, patches of his skin were freezer burned, gray and bloodless, like an old forgotten piece of liver no one wanted to eat. "Fuck," said Mal.

"I think Rip was right. We should have minded our own business and stayed the fuck out of here."

"Close this thing and let's get the hell out of here."

They sat down across the table from Rip, his face hidden behind a music magazine, Blue Suede News. He lowered the magazine about two inches, looked at their gloomy faces, "And?" he asked.

"Well, now we know what she's been doing in the shed," said Ktel.

Rip said nothing, simply continued staring at them over his magazine.

"She's digging a hole through the concrete floor," said Mal

"Mm-hmm," Rip lowered the magazine and set it on the table.

"Most likely to hide what's being hidden in the freezer," said Mal.

"What are the odds," said Ktel. "We randomly pick a place in the middle of the desert to hide out, and it just happens to be the place where some old lady is hiding a body."

"You found a body?" asked Rip. "Like a dead body?"

"In the freezer," said Mal. "Thinking about it, that's the first dead body I've seen in my whole life."

"Man. Ray's gonna be pissed," said Rip. He stood, opened the fridge and took out a beer.

Copa Girl

"Fuck! What the hell were you guys thinking?" said Ray, his voice growing more strained, and the tempo of his breath picking up.

"Ray," said Ktel, "better to know than not know. We're not even sure who's in the freezer. I'm guessing her husband. What if someone comes around looking for him—maybe even some local cop? Everybody knows everybody in these hick places."

"Probably best to split, find a new place to hang," said Rip.

No one felt like firing up the grill so Ray stuck four chicken pot pies in the microwave oven.

They were sitting around outside after dinner when the Babbitts rolled by, their Streamline hooked to the back of the truck. Sheryl stuck her head out of the passenger window. "Hey y'all, just wanted to wish you luck on the rest of the tour." She slid her hand out the window next to her head and gave them a wave.

"You heading out?" asked Ray.

"Yep," said Sheryl. "Our casino luck's run-dry. We're heading back up North."

"Have a safe drive," said Ray, holding his beer can up in a salute.

A glowing burst of sunset was exploding over the western ridge of the campground. "That's beautiful," said Mal.

"Yeah she is," said Rip. They were all sitting outside, Ray and Ktel on the campsite's picnic table, Rip and Mal in fold-out chairs. Over dinner they had unanimously decided to head deeper into Arizona. They'd leave first thing after breakfast.

Polly startled them, popping out of the dark from around the camper. "Evening. Stopping by to see how all the guests are doing. Anything I can help you folks with?"

"Naw. We're good," said Ray.

"Mind if I sit a spell with ya?"

"Sure Polly," said Mal. "Rip, get the lady a beer."

Polly sat down on the end of the bench next to Ray. "With the Babbitts gone, it's just y'all left." Rip came back and handed her a can of beer. She cracked the top open and took a small sip, mostly foam. "Thanks. Appreciate it. Been parched all day.

Yep. Slow out here this time of the year, sometimes go weeks without a customer—can get pretty lonely now that Cesar's gone."

"Huhummgh," Mal cleared her throat.

Polly looked up at Mal. They made eye contact, although only a brief moment, it felt like minutes for Mal.

"I know y'all found out about Cesar. Someone was snoopin' around the shed today while I was in town, even got into the freezer."

The camp suddenly became very quiet, which amplified the crackling of the wood in the firepit.

"I'm not sure what y'all are planning to do about it. If you'd already called the cops, I guess they'd be around by now. Maybe you're still planning to call the cops, whatever you're planning to do, I'm only asking for a few minutes of your time to tell my side of it."

No one from the band said anything. Rip picked up his beer, took a healthy swallow, set it back down and leaned forward over the table closer to Polly.

Polly took a deep breath through her nose, exhaled, looked around at each member of the band, and began telling her story:

"Look around the place," said Polly, holding her arms out, palms up. "The place has run its course, old, like me, not a lot of time left." Polly paused, took a drink. "Cesar, he was my man, and he had been for quite some time. I loved him. I still do. But he was a stubborn old Mexican, wanted to sell—just got the nine acres left here, used to be twenty. We had to sell a few here, a few there, pay off the taxes and the bank."

Polly paused and looked out into the dark. She pointed with her finger. "Right there, on that little mound, where the showers are now. If you look closely, you can still see where the foundation was, used to be a little inn there, all along the bottom of the hill there. A U.S. Senator bought this land and built the inn back in nineteen-thirty, and named it The Pittman Inn. He knew the dam was coming, and there'd be a lot of politicians, businessmen coming-and-a-going—Boulder City weren't no place for men like these, that's where all the laborers lived. No, they'd need their own place, but a place close by, and the Senator was there to supply it. Hoover Dam was coming and everybody was cashing in on it."

"My daddy, Otis Lloyd, he came out here for the dam, too. He was only nineteen years old. He tramped, jumped the trains, and walked all the way from Oklahoma—that was back in nineteen-thirty one." Polly stopped, took a slow and careful drink from her beer, rubbed her eyes, and continued.

"He didn't come alone. Twenty-one thousand able-bodied young men came from all over the country. It was the depression, and there were a lot of folks out of work. Before they got around to building up housing for the workers in Boulder City, most of the workers lived right up next to the building site in Ragtown, a giant camp of tents, cardboard boxes, scrap, whatever they could find to cover their heads from the scorching heat of the desert."

"My daddy used to tell me the stories. All those men, hauling rocks, pouring concrete, busting their asses, all in the hottest damn place on earth. They'd get paid every Friday at quitting time—cash. They could sit around their sweltering tents in Ragtown or they could hop on one of the trucks that would take them into Vegas. The trucks would drop them right off at the end of Fremont Street. Casinos, booze, and women, what more could a man want." Polly smiled, took a drink, and then gave her can a shake, "All this talking is making me thirsty, drank that beer right up." Without a word, Ktel, being closest to the camper door, jumped up and got Polly another beer.

"My daddy quickly found his calling, he took to the old Fremont casinos like a fist to an eye. He was one of the top Five-Card Stud players in his day—Lucky Hand Lloyd they called him. He wasn't three months working on the dam, when he decided to quit and dedicate himself full time to the poker tables."

"It was in Forty-five, my daddy told me, he was playing in a high-stakes game of stud poker in the back room of the Monte Carlo; he took the Senator for all the money he had on him and the deed to the twenty acres, including the inn. It wasn't worth much at the time, the dam had been finished for ten years; it was sitting empty, getting sun-bleached out in this torrid canyon."

"He met mama a year later. Mama was named after the actress Fay Wray. She was seventeen when she met Otis. They got married right after she turned eighteen—six months later I arrived."

"The Sands Hotel opened in nineteen-fifty-two and mama got a job there as a showgirl. She was one of the original Copa girls, and she worked at the Sands until the day she died."

"I grew up in downtown Las Vegas. We had a nice place six blocks from Fremont Street. Being a kid in Vegas in the fifties was special, but we didn't know that then; we were only kids. I remember them lining us all up outside of the school so we could watch the mushroom clouds from the nuclear bomb testing. Those fantastic clouds would rise up over the horizon to the northwest, we thought they were beautiful. They gave us celluloid glasses to protect our eyes. Once some soldiers, all spiffy in their uniforms, came by the school with nurses, took blood samples, gave each one of us dog tags to wear around our necks, told us how patriotic we were.

And then the sixties came, Vietnam, The Kennedy assassinations. When I was seventeen, my best friend, Jane and I hitchhiked to California. It was the first time I had seen the ocean. We traveled up the coast, got caught up in the whole sixties movement. We were living in San Francisco when I met Cesar—he was strong, dark, and handsome. He was a hell of a guitar player too. I remember sitting down in Golden Gate Park, how he could swoon me with his guitar and his exotic accent."

"I think it was sixty-eight, my uncle tracked me down, told me both daddy and mama were killed in a car accident. Daddy had picked up mama when she got off work at the Sands, they were driving down Paradise Avenue when a car full of drunken college students swerved over into their lane."

"Cesar and I came back to Vegas, had a funeral, and buried my folks at Woodlawn Cemetery. They left me a little savings and twenty acres in the middle of the desert, including the run-down inn."

"We drove out here and set up house in the old inn. Two weeks later, I called Jane who was still in San Francisco working at the *I & Thou* coffee house. A week later she came rolling down the road in a small bus along with eight other Haight-Ashbury freaks. And oh lordy, we had ourselves our very own free-thinking, Bohemian commune in the middle of the desert."

"All this hippie talk's making me wanna twist one up," Rip got up and went for his stash.

"I never liked the word hippie," said Polly. "I always preferred *freak*."

"Wanna another beer," asked Mal.

"Ain't gonna say no." Polly laughed, everyone joined in on it.

"Where was I? Yes, the *Desert Inn*. We changed the name from the *Pittman Inn* to the *Desert Inn*.

One of the guys even climbed up on a ladder and repainted the old sign. Hell, most of the people who crashed here were proclaimed artists, musicians or poets. It weren't no time, the inn was covered in murals and paintings, even a sculpture or two were decorating the grounds. Freaks, mostly from California, were coming and going—it was a never-ending party."

"Sounds like it was pretty badass," said Rip. He lit the joint he had finished rolling, took a deep hit, and handed it over to Polly.

"Yes, it was a hell of a time," Polly nodded her head, took a hit from the joint, passed it over to Ray, and coughed up a large cloud of smoke. She looked sternly into Rip's eyes. "But all parties must end. And that one ended in a blaze of glory."

"It was February, seventy-one, not two months after the Altamont concert. There was this one guy from LA." Polly paused, looked up. "I can't remember his name now. But I'll never forget what he looked like, short, dark curly hair, and black mangy sideburns that covered a good part of his face, dark little eyes that peered out of deep sunken sockets. He had only been here a week. He showed up with some grass and a good supply of LSD. A lot of folks were tripping that night, I wasn't, I had just come down the day before and wasn't ready to go back up again. I heard he was up to three hit trips, went off the rails, and started the inn on fire. I'm not even sure what happened, I had been sitting outside, listening to Cesar and some girl playing guitar and singing.

Next thing we knew, the whole building was on fire, the few people who were inside, ran out. The sideburns guy was the last one to make it out. I'll never forget the look on his face, eyes blazing, his lips pulled back in a mad grin. He ran out, and he just kept running, ran over the ridge there and was gone. We never saw him again." Polly stopped her narrative and took a long pull off her beer.

"And that was the end of the party," said Ray.

"Yes it was, in less than a week everybody had drifted away, probably back to California, left just Cesar and me. The little adobe house there hadn't been used in years, had been the service quarters back in the dam-building days. We had been using it for spare parts for the inn. Well, we fixed it up, made it livable. It was Cesar's idea to make the campground—and it was a good idea. We ran the campground for decades; we had the hikers and the rafters, still a trail over there that goes down to the river." Polly pointed in the direction the Babbitts had been parked. "Cesar had even built a nice little boat landing for the rafters. We never made a lot of money, but we kept our heads above water and life was good. We were happy." Polly looked off into the distance. The band sat quietly, waiting for the end of the story. Polly smiled and continued.

"The Arizona Department of State Parks built the Wili Campground a few more miles down the highway—beautiful modern sites, information center, boat rentals, guided tours, that was the beginning of the end for us."

"We struggled. We struggled and fought for the last fifteen years to keep this place going. We sold off over half the land to the State Park, they're just waiting for me to die so they can get the rest."

"Cesar wanted to sell. He wanted to sell and move down to Mexico, said he had some family down in Mexico City. With the money we got from this place we'd be able to retire on down there." Polly blinked, looked around at the band. "Any of you folks got a cigarette? I ain't had a cigarette in years."

"Sorry. Don't smoke," said Ray.

"Some weed now-and-again," added Rip.

"Nobody smokes anymore." Polly took another good pull off her beer, the joint had made her thirsty. "I thought about it. I really did. Moving to Mexico. Do you know how many people live in Mexico City? A lot, I looked it up, millions! I've been living out here most of my life now—Cesar and me. And I'm too old to learn Spanish. This little patch of sand, rock, and cacti is the only thing I've got from my daddy. I wanted to die here. Whatever time I've got left, I'd like to live it right here."

"We fought, and we fought, and we fought some more, that went on for a couple of years. Cesar said we'd lose it all, wind up without a pan to fry roadkill in, better to sell now, while we can. Hell, he was probably right. We'd end up living in the drainage tunnels under Las Vegas. But I couldn't, I just couldn't, this is my home, been here since my folks passed, I plan to pass here, too."

"One day, we had just finished breakfast, we got into it bad. He said he was going to sell half the place and move to Mexico without me. He yelled, I yelled. He grabbed me and pushed me up against the counter hard. I don't know, I guess the devil got into me. I picked up the cast-iron skillet I had just dried and hit him on the head with it. He went down without a blink." Tears were running down Polly's checks, but she continued on.

"I fell on the floor with him. I shook him, I slapped his face, tried to wake him up. But I knew, I knew he was gone. Finally, I just laid with him. I laid there with him for a long time. Hours later, the phone rang. I got up and answered it, someone calling to reserve a campsite. I took the reservation, politely, hung up the phone, and somehow dragged Cesar back to the shed and got him into the freezer."

"This might not be the time to ask," said Rip, "but why bury him under the shed, there's a million miles of desert out here?"

Polly lowered her eyebrows, "A coyote, or some other critter might dig him up. I couldn't have that, he's my man, and I wanted him here with me."

"Sorry, no disrespect."

"Well," said Polly, wiping the last tears off her cheeks. "I said my peace, y'all can do what you want now."

Ray looked around at the band. Rip tilted his head and smiled at him. One of the greatest things about playing in a truly tight band, the keen-subtle communication between its members. After years of working together on stage: a brief glance, a nod, a slight movement, told the others exactly what you had in mind—no words required.

"I got a twelve-pound sledge and a tarp. We'll be able to break up the rest of the floor, Rip and I can get the whole job done in an hour or two." said Ktel.

Polly's eyes darted from one band member to the next, "I don't understand. Are y'all gonna help me lay my Cesar to rest."

"Yes ma'am, but in the morning," said Ray. He stood and walked into the camper.

Lo mío es tuyo

The next morning, Mal made some toasted waffles for breakfast. After eating, and a third cup of coffee, Rip and Ktel went to work in the shed. At noon, Polly brought over a big pot of chili she had made. She poured out a bowl for each person, sprinkled some raw onion and grated yellow-cheese on top.

"That's good," said Rip, "just the right amount of fire in it."

"I talked to one of the twins," said Ray, between spoonfuls of chili. "Rip and I need to run a little errand. Ktel can you finish up the floor?"

"Yeah, gotta mix up a batch of concrete, two hours, tops."

"Polly, we're gonna need your truck."

Polly smiled and nodded. "I'll get the keys." She got up and headed back to the house.

"Some good news," Ray looked up from his bowl. "Billy's out of jail and being snuck out of Vegas as we speak."

Mal's eyes widened. "Is he on the way here?"

"No. Too risky. He's outta jail, but not out of harm's way yet," said Ray. "They're bringing him straight to the ranch."

"The ranch?" asked Rip.

"He'll be safe there." Ray set his bowl on the table and stood up. "I reckon we can pick him up on our way home."

B Before C

Ray took a right on Highway 93 heading south. "What's the plan?" asked Rip.

"Have to meet a guy down in Phoenix." said Ray. "Gotta pick up a wrecked station wagon, tow it back up to Searchlight, a town fifty miles south of Vegas."

"All right."

"It's time to get Billy out of this mess."

At just past two, Ray and Rip pulled up behind a junkyard on the outskirts of Searchlight Nevada.

They were in the cab of a Chevrolet Kodiak flatbed tow truck pulling a Ford Focus. The car was totaled, the entire right-front of it was completely smashed in. It looked like it had hit a telephone pole. Rip jumped out of the passenger side, walked to the back, Ray lowered the hoist, and Rip unhitched it.

A window blind opened in the rear of the large metal building that was in front of the junkyard. A large bearded man wearing boxers and a stained wife-beater shirt peered out at the tow truck dropping off the wrecked car. He shrugged, scratched his crotch, and flopped back down on the couch he had been sleeping on.

The Twins

A late-model Jeep Cherokee pulled up in front of the ranch house. It was a big timber house sitting on top of a stone foundation. The stones were from the original foundation of the old house which burned down in 1963. Six years ago, Dan had bought the land, all four-hundred acres of it, including what was left of the charred foundation. It was located on the western slopes of Colorado, eight miles from the town of Hotchkiss. The house sat on top of a slight basin, creating a panoramic view from the front porch of the entire bottom of the valley below.

Doug stepped out of the Jeep and walked up the steps leading to the front porch. Dan opened the door and came out to greet him. Although twins, they weren't identical. Doug was five-ten, a roundish tear-drop face sitting on top of a slight build. He wore jeans, a flannel shirt with red suspenders, and a sturdy pair of work boots. He looked like a Northern Woods lumberjack. Dan, on the other hand , was a cowboy. He stood about six-two, had a lean, fit body, wore cowboy boots, a gray country-western shirt, and he often kept a stetson perched on top of his head. But brothers they were;

they both had the same thick dirty-blond hair and deep-sunken pale blue eyes.

Doug stood there, his road weary-eyes blinking up at his brother. Doug seldom started a conversation and was the flip-side of Dan's easy-going, sociable nature.

Dan stepped up and hugged his brother. "Howdy brother. How was the drive?"

"They popped me for twenty-over on Interstate 80 going through Nebraska—I fucking hate Nebraska, a big long fucking speeding trap."

"Come on in. I got some Coors chilling on ice."

"Are you still drinking that mountain piss-water? I knew I should have brought some real beer down with me."

After feeding Doug a flank steak, the two brothers sat out on the porch drinking beer.

"Nice view, but I couldn't live down here, too fucking dry and empty."

"When I'm out riding, and you see miles of the horizon with no trace of humans, well, that's something special."

Doug looked squarely at his brother. "What are we gonna do about this fuck-up?"

"Don't you worry, Dougie. I got us a plan, it's already in motion, sweep the whole thing under the rug."

"I said it was a mistake getting Ray for the job, they're fucking musicians, we should have gotten pros."

"Hey! Weren't their fault, it was bad intel. How many jobs has he done for us till now? How many times have they fucked up? They're the tightest crew we've got. No one knew about the second alarm. If it's anyone's fault, it's our guys down in Vegas. Anyway, fuck it. Can't change the past, we move forward."

"Chicago is gonna be pissed, they wanted this clean. They wanted Delbowski guessing, turn up the heat between the Polish and the bikers."

"I know what the plan was, and like I said, shit happens, we move forward. Besides, I think Chicago's gonna like my new plan. If it works out the way I think it will, the Polish and the bikers will be all over each other."

"If Delbowski's guys pick up the bass player, he'll sing like a Jackson."

Dan smiled at his brother. "Don't worry, man. He should be getting out of jail as we speak, and it ain't gonna be the Polish who pick him up, cause the Vego will snatch him up first."

Doug leaned forward, his eyes widened. "And how the fuck is that better?"

"Relax brother. It's Jake and Fury wearing Vego colors. It's all part of the plan."

"Sounds like a cluster fuck," said Doug, "more things that can wrong, the bigger chance something will go wrong."

"You got a better idea, brother?"

"Maybe." Doug leaned back in his chair. "If they can't find the bass player …?" He shrugged and took a drink of beer.

Dan turned to look in Doug's face, his eyes narrowed, "That'll just make them suspicious. They'll hunt down the whole band."

Doug said nothing, just shrugged again.

"Dude. This is Ray we're talking about. Ray goes way back. Are you forgetting what happened up in Two Harbors? He saved our asses up there."

Doug leaned forward again, held his hands out, palms up. "Look around Danny. You got a nice spread here, business is good, our networks are strong. You got Lori back, man." He took a drink, leaned even closer into his brother. "Are you ready to put it all on the line, because this thing is a powder keg waiting to blow up in our faces."

Dan leaned even closer in, his face inches from his brother's. "Turn around brother. Turn around, walk to the top of shut-the-fuck-up mountain and enjoy the view, but quietly."

The Vegas Job
Part III

After an hour in the holding cell, they questioned me for another hour, asked me the same questions they had asked the night they arrested me. I told them the same story: the backstage girl, the party, the building in North Vegas across from the cemetery. I walked into the building; no one was around; it was as dead as the damned in there. Either I was in the wrong place, or that girl had been yanking my chain. I turned around and split. I didn't get more than a few feet when you guys were trying to run me down.

At six o'clock they cut me loose. regrettably, they took the Vonnegut book from me—I would have liked to read it.

I left the building by the rear entrance, which led to the parking ramp. I found myself standing in an alley between the ramp and the jail house; there was only one way to go. I walked out of the alley onto the downtown street.

A black Mercedes Benz S-Class sat in a parking lot across 1st Street on the next corner. The two men sitting in the car had a clear view of where the alley opened onto the street. Both men were dressed in expensive designer jogging outfits, both wore Berluti sneakers, both men wore their hair short and slicked straight back tight over their skulls, both men looked conspicuously gangster. "There's our guy," said the man behind the wheel. He started the motor. "Let's let him get a block from the station before we pick him up."

He put the car into reverse and was backing out when his partner said, "Wait. I think we got trouble."

A brown delivery van swooped to the curb as soon as I walked out on the street. The passenger door flew open and a sizeable dude in black leather biker pants and patched vest was right on me. I recognized him; it was the same dude from the jail who was looking for a smoke.

My mind raced to process what-the-fuck was going on when the side door of the van slid open - his partner was waiting inside. The firs guy bulldozed me backwards into the van. I flung my arms out and grabbed onto the door frame. I tried to lunge my body forward; I was just gaining some forward momentum when the heel of his hand hit me in the forehead and I was catapulted back into the van, and the guy inside grabbed me and hurled me like a rag doll further back into the van. The biker outside slid the door shut and jumped into the front of the van. The black dude hopped forward into the driver's seat and shot back into the downtown traffic.

I spun myself over, still a little dizzy from getting slugged in the head.

The white guy turned and leaned into the rear of the van. He held his hand up, palm out. "Relax Billy. It's all show. Two of Delbowski's guys were waiting to pick your ass up. The twins sent us to save you. My name's Jake, and this here's Fury."

The two men in the Mercedes sat passively and watched the van take off down the street.

"The boss ain't gonna like this shit." said the one behind the wheel.

"Fuck no," said his partner. "I hate those fucking bikers."

"This shit's gonna get nasty."

"Yep."

Fabian

Fabian Delbowski sat behind his desk, a solid round whiskey glass in his right hand. The gold-framed plaque hung empty on the wall behind his head like a bad omen. Fabian looked more stockbroker than gangster; he was lean from spending five days a week in the gym, had an expensive cutting edge haircut, and if it weren't for the nasty scar running down his left cheek, he had boyish good looks. "Why the fuck didn't you go after them and snatch the bass player?" Fabian asked, calmly and lucidly.

The two goons stood in front of Fabian's desk, the bigger of the two replied. "What could we have done, boss? Start a shootout in downtown Las Vegas. Like I said, we followed them all the way to Boulder City where they got on 95 South—nothing down there but Searchlight. We turned around, came straight back here."

Fabian stared up at them, expressionless. For the people who knew him, that's when you get nervous. "Are you sure they were wearing Vego patches?"

"Absofuckinglutely, boss."

Fabian stared down at the black leather blotter on his desk.

The bigger goon spoke again, "You want us to get a couple more guys boss, drive down there, stake out the place, see what we can see."

Fabian looked up at him with a curious, subtle sense of awe on his face. After an excruciating pause, he spoke. "Are you a fucking moron, or what? If you get anywhere near Searchlight, those bikers will make you in a second."

"It was just an idea, boss."

"I ain't paying you for ideas." Fabian turned his head and looked over at Lucas Bennett, his lawyer and long-time business associate. Lucas stood in the corner next to a vintage liquor cabinet. He was short, wore a suit that had been obsolete for a decade, had a balding head, and a thin wispy mustache that lived above his white lifeless lips. Regardless of how he looked, Lucas was a fierce litigator in the courtroom, and Fabian trusted him more than his own brother. Lucas claimed to be the great-grandson of Granville Bennett, a lawyer and the first elected judge of the infamous town of Deadwood, South Dakota. "Why would these scumbag bikers steal my Hendrix guitar?"

Lucas shrugged and took a sip of the whiskey he had poured. "Damned if I know. They could sell it, but only to some rich idiot that wants to hide it in his basement forever. Maybe someone paid them to steal it, but it doesn't feel like that, feels like they're sending a message."

"And what the fuck's with the musician? We

want to pick him up, push him a little harder than the cops, find out if he knows anything, and the fucking Vego snatch him up—right out from under us?"

"That got us by surprise too, boss," said the bigger goon. The smaller goon still hadn't spoken, just stood next to his partner and rolled back-and-forth on the balls of his feet.

"Don't you two have someplace to be?" Fabian asked.

"Sure thing boss." the two goons spun in unison and walked out the door.

As soon as the door closed, Lucas continued, "They got a few cops on the payroll, same as us. It wouldn't be hard for them to find out when they released the guy. What I can't figure is, why would they want him? According to our guys, he was just some schmuck at the wrong place, at the wrong time. His story checked out, a bass player from some country band out of Ponopolis. They played that night at some redneck place on Fremont. The idiot was wandering around the building looking for a party."

"Could be they were worried he saw something," said Fabian. "I thought we had an understanding with the Vego. I thought we had solid lines drawn up. We're all making money. Why start trouble?"

"Not a clue," said Lucas. "I guess you'll have to ask them."

"I called down there an hour ago and spoke to the

Kingpin himself. He claims not to know anything." Fabian took a drink of whiskey and set his glass down on a solid-stone coaster. "How many guys can we get together in a hurry? I don't want a war, but the only thing those bikers understand is a show of force."

An hour later someone knocked on the door. Fabian pushed a button under the edge of his desk and buzzed them in. It was the bigger goon again. "I got a guy out here. I think you'll want to hear what he has to say."

Fabian waved his hand, gesturing to send the guy in. A lanky man with stiff hair and a long nose walked in. He looked like a giant underfed rooster.

"What do you got?"

"Last night, I picked up a rumor," he spoke in a high nasal voice, "about a stolen guitar, and where it might be."

Fabian looked up at him, "and why bring this to me? Don't tell me you're a good Samaritan."

"I got a big number out with one of your bookies. I can barely keep up on the juice. Maybe we can help each other out?"

"How big is the number?" asked Fabian.

Searchlight

The convoy pulled off Highway 95 and took a left on Cottonwood Cove Road. Searchlight is a bone-dry town in the Southern corner of Nevada. It's a living ghost town with rusty old derelict structures from the gold mining boom strewn between occupied trailers and houses. The town is also home to the Vego, a notorious motorcycle club that controls Southern Nevada, Northwestern Arizona, and Southwestern California. The Vego are a desert motorcycle club dating back to the late nineteen-fifties. Although they ran the two casinos in Searchlight, the bulk of their business was drugs and guns with a little fencing and pornography on the side. The club's founder, Snake Ziegler, died in the early seventies and the club has since had three presidents—the current one was Brennan Dougal, AKA Kingpin.

Fabian sat in the backseat of his Mercedes, which led a convoy of twenty men in five vehicles. He knew a direct confrontation with the bikers in their town wasn't the best strategy, but after finding out they had his guitar and where they were hiding it, he would make a move. Fucking mystified at why they took it, it pissed him off. He knew now wasn't the time to appear weak, the bikers would start crossing like hyenas into his business. He'd learned that Chicago had a fresh eye on Vegas and were looking for a foothold. His father had left Jersey and come out here to the desert in nineteen-seventy. He was smart, worked hard, fought and carved out a place for himself in Las Vegas. Fabian started working for his father when he was fifteen and since his old man died, had been running the organization. No, he wouldn't let the bikers or anyone else move in on him. He would fight if he had to.

The convoy turned right on Colorado Street; they crossed Hobson Street and drove onto an unpaved road kicking up dirt and gravel. Fabian could see the Vego's headquarters coming into view. There was a large structure of corrugated steel, several smaller structures, and about half a dozen mobile homes were parked in a cluster south of the main building. There was a scrapyard behind everything which they used for spare parts and where the local sheriff's office dumped all the wrecks from the highway accidents. The Vego ran a service center that repaired cars, trucks and motorcycles at cut-rate prices for the small local population—it was good PR.

The main building itself was fronted with five work bays with offices and storage to the right. The club's headquarters was located in the rear, a bar with a pool table and vintage pinball machine. Next to that was a three-bedroom apartment, with a whirlpool and sauna, where the President and his current old lady lived.

Fabian and his top guys had studied the layout of the place on Google Maps. At this time of day there probably weren't more than ten bikers at their headquarters. Many of the club members lived in

Searchlight and someone would call in as soon as they spotted the convoy. He hoped to catch them vulnerable, get his Hendrix back, and get his ass back to Vegas.

His car pulled into the lot first, the second car parked on his left, the third to the right. The SUV and the van parked behind the front cars at a slight angle—it was a formation. Everyone but the driver stepped out of Fabian's car, several men stepped out of the wing cars, but no one exited the rear vehicles.

Fabian and his men walked out in front of his Mercedes. They didn't have to wait long, a door in the front of the main structure opened and Kingpin himself walked out into the lot with two more bikers in tow. Kingpin looked like he'd stepped out of a time machine. He was a replica of any biker you could drag out of any sixties biker movie, from *The Wild One* to *The Wild Angels*. He was big, with a massive beard, biker boots, the leather vest over his dark-red shirt was emblazoned with patches and emblems, including the simple patch above the cigarette pocket that read, *President*.

"What can we do for you today?" His voice matched his appearance. He sounded like a rusty tuba, but oddly, resonating in low soothing melody.

"Look." Fabian took a step closer toward the bikers. "War isn't good business, not for anyone. But taking my guitar, that's personal." A half-dozen bikers rode into the lot behind him, and a few more had come around the corner from the trailers. Their odds were going down fast.

"What the fuck's with you and this guitar. I told you on the phone, no Vego jacked your guitar. If one did, and didn't tell me, well, he'd be a Vego no more." The big man folded his arms. "You think you can show up here, at our home, with a fucking army—uninvited."

"I want the guitar. I've reason to believe it's here."

"And I'm saying, it ain't here." Kingpin shrugged his shoulders, looked around the lot, more bikers were showing up.

"Nobody wants trouble, Brennan. But I have to be sure; then we'll split." Fabian caught a sound from behind the nearest garage bay door.

The Kingpin scowled, shook his head. "Only my lady calls me Brennan." He reached into his pocket and pulled out a large keyring and tossed it on the ground. "This place here. This has belonged to Vego for three generations." Kingpin looked at Fabian in the eyes. "You come here. Call me a liar, a sneak thief. You wanna paw through my things, disrespect my home." He pointed down to his keys. "There you go, take my keys. Take my bike, my home, take it all." Kingpin put his hands on his hips, chest out. "But you're gonna have to take it over my dead fucking body." His right hand reached behind his back and he pulled out a Smith and Wesson 500; a long fifteen inch barrel of dissolution.

For Fabian, time seemed to slow down. He could see Kingpin's hand coming up in a slower-than-life motion. Kingpin's eyes never left Fabian's. His arm swung a little to the right. BOOM! He saw the side of a man's head explode. A man that worked for him, a man that wasn't yet thirty. He had a wife, a house in Paradise near the airport.

And then time started changing its direction, like a rubber band that had been wound too tight. The world around him was speeding up; flying into action.

Fabian jumped back and took cover behind the fender of his car. Kingpin turned and started walking back to the door he had come out of a minute ago; walking like he had all the time in the world, burdenless to the chaos he had set in motion at his back. The two men who had followed him, sprung out front to cover their President, both had pulled out handguns and were blasting away at Fabian and his men.

The nearest bay door flew up, heavy steel and wood boxes had been stacked up, and several bikers began firing assault rifles from behind them. Fabian's men were pouring out of the vehicles and firing back. Fabian heard the M60 burst into action. They had set it up in the back of the van, the gunner protected by sandbags.

Guns are much louder in real-life than in the movies, Fabian couldn't hear anything but the high-pitched ringing in his ears. He had his Desert Eagle out and at least three of his rounds had struck center-mass into one of the bikers covering Kingpin's retreat. The headlamp, inches from Fabian's head, exploded sending glass fragments into his face. He jumped further back behind his car while firing over the hood.

The wall tore up as rounds struck next to the door the Kingpin was walking through. His shoulder flinched and then he was swallowed up by the building.

One of Fabian's men ran over and was firing over his head at some bikers who were coming around the building from the other direction. Fabian scrambled on his hands and knees to the back of the car and popped the trunk open. He tossed his handgun aside and pulled out an AK-47 and several magazines. He popped the lid on a metal ammo box and took out a Soviet F1 hand grenade.

He turned and saw the war going on behind him. His men were concentrated in the center of the vehicles shooting outward. He saw at least five bikers down near the gate. The M60 was still blasting away out the back of the van.

He pulled the pin on the grenade but kept the lever suppressed. Still squatting, he made his way closer to the front of the car. He took one look through the windows and lobbed the grenade over the car; it struck the ground near the entrance to the first bay door of the workshop and rolled inside.

"DOWN!" shouted Fabian. He got down tighter behind the car, he didn't have to wait long. WOOOM! The ground underneath Fabian shifted a fraction of an inch. His car bounced back on its shocks as shrapnel pounded into the other side of it.

The first two bays in the workshop were destroyed and something had caught fire. A fire extinguisher was going off inside, and some of his men were still shooting in that direction.

Fabian raised his head and looked around. The bikers coming in through the gate from town hadn't stood a chance against the M60 in the van. There was no good cover, the survivors must have retreated back they way they'd come. He saw a few people down on the right near the trailers; nothing was moving there now. He had no idea how many were still inside, and had no intention of going in there to find out.

He stood up straight and held his hand in the air to signal his men to stop firing. The door directly in front of his car exploded outward as Kingpin, armed with a double-barreled shotgun, charged through it. Fabian dropped to one knee and let go half a magazine from his AK. At least half the rounds hit meat, Kingpin began falling forward shooting off both barrels on the way to the ground; most of the pellets hit the ground in front of the car but a few struck Fabian's left shin and foot. But he felt nothing, the adrenaline in his veins was turned up to the max. He stood up, flipped a new magazine into his weapon, and signaled to two of his men to follow.

The three men went around the main building to the left. They held their weapons high and kept a close watch on the windows, or any place someone could shoot from. A biker was lying up against the wall around the corner. He was holding his leg with both hands, blood was pumping out between his fingers. He was moaning, his face covered in sweat. Fabian let off one round, it struck him beside his temple and a good portion of the back of his skull splattered onto the cinder brick wall. They made their way back to the boneyard, walking slow and vigilant through the yard, careful of anyone who might be hiding in or behind one of the wrecks.

He found it in the last row, a red Ford Focus. Its entire front end destroyed. He walked around to the rear hatch door; it was locked. One of his men reached into the front and popped open the rear door. He set down his weapon, reached inside and opened the compartment under the floor where the spare tire was usually stored.

And there it was, a black guitar bag. He unzipped it, looked at the guitar, and zipped it back up. He slung the bag over his shoulder and started walking back out of the junkyard.

Of Mice and Friends

Lizzie stroked him. Brock was leaning back on the couch; his sunken eyes were dark slits. A deep moan came from his chest every time she touched him. With her other hand, she began caressing his scrotum. His entire body quivered under her touch and that turned her on.

She stopped to pull off her t-shirt, a black tight-fitting girl's cut with the words Plant Power printed in bold red letters across her breast. She wasn't wearing a bra, and she could see Brock's eyes following her small pale breasts like a hypnotist's watch. She slipped out of her jeans and underwear, kneeled back down and began stroking him again.

Lizzie was a petite girl, she wore her blonde hair short and butch which highlighted her large dark green eyes. People were often misled by her stature, she had a small body but a larger-than-life character and a deep loud, demanding voice. She bent forward and put the tip of his member in her mouth while pumping the shaft slowly with her right hand. He was throbbing, his crescendo building, but she didn't want him to ejaculate—not yet.

She stopped. Brock's eyes opened a little wider. Lizzie climbed up on the couch and straddled him. She was wet and had no trouble slipping him inside. She began rocking slowly back and forth.

Lizzie picked up the tempo. Brock's back straightened. He reached up and cupped her breast in his hand. He was trying to hold back but was quickly losing the battle. Brock's back arched up pushing himself deeper inside her. He clutched both of her shoulders and let out a muffled wail. Lizzie's upper body swung forward, she grabbed two handfuls of Brock's hair and pulled his head into her breasts. He wrapped his arms around her; they lay locked together for several minutes until their muscles started to relax and Lizzie gently slid off to the side.

They lay panting, half on the couch, half on the floor. They were in Brock's basement apartment. He rented it from his mother who lived upstairs. Brock was twenty years old, six feet tall, jet black hair which hung down to his shoulders. He was a part-time student at a local community college and worked at a local radio station selling advertising spots to local businesses. The apartment was a long narrow room which ran the length of the house. A small open kitchen with an island counter was at the end of the room. A door next to the kitchen led to a small bathroom with a toilet, sink, and shower. The rest of the basement was a utility room with a washer and dryer that Brock and his mother shared.

The wall on the opposite end of the kitchen was the most dominating thing in the room. It was painted matte black with a thick round circle painted from floor to ceiling. There was a large A painted in the center of the circle. Most people who entered the room for the first time assumed it was the well-known Anarchist symbol, on closer inspection they would notice the black lettering, Animal Liberation, written in the top-center of the circle over the A, and Front under the A. The two walls that ran the length of the basement were covered in a collage of posters - band posters which spanned the last forty years from The Dead Kennedys to My Chemical Romance, animal rights posters depicting horrific scenes of animals being slaughtered and mishandled. Above the couch, rows of concert tickets were tacked to the wall like trophies. Across from the couch was a low-board, the top littered with a stack of aging stereo components, CDs, magazines, and a large flat screen TV.

"Is your mom home?"

"Don't know. Why?"

"I think we were louder than usual."

"I don't know what shift she's got this week, but when she's home, she's either all wined up on Pinot and watching one of her lame-ass reality shows, or sleeping like a fermenting grape."

"You shouldn't talk like that about your mom. Besides, she is your landlady she could kick you out."

"She knows she drinks too much wine, and she knows the shows she's hooked on are total crap, but it winds her down after a long shift at the hospital." Brock sat up and started searching for his boxers. "I pray every day that no one shows her how social media works; she'd be mainlining memes in a week."

One Hour Later

Brock and Lizzie lay entwined on the couch watching The Wrestler on DVD.

"I've always liked Mickey Rourke," said Brock.

"Yeah. Have you ever seen Rumble Fish?" asked Lizzie.

Brock carefully slid Lizzie's leg over and sat up. "I don't think so. How old is it?"

"It's a classic, man. You have to watch it. It's got Mickey Rourke, Matt Dillon, and Dennis Hopper's in it, too."

"Sounds bad ass. Let's rent it sometime." Although, they had just met nine days ago, Brock was falling hard for Lizzie. He'd had several girlfriends in the past, but nothing with this kind of connection; she had a great taste in music and movies.

He started sliding stuff around on the coffee

table, magazines, bank statements, junk mail, and a two-day-old pizza box.

"Don't have to rent it. I got it on DVD. I'll bring it over sometime. What are you looking for?"

"The joint." He found it in the ashtray on the floor between the coffee table and the couch. He picked it up. "Still a few good hits left on it." He leaned forward and looked around on the floor. "Shit. Have you seen the lighter?"

They both looked up. Someone was thumping down the stairs.

"Gill," said Brock.

They heard someone try the doorknob and then knock.

"Coming," shouted Brock. He got up and opened the door. "Dude" and sat back down on the couch before the door opened entirely.

"Dude." Gill walked in. He was a good foot shorter than Brock, curly brown hair, and though he was the same age as Brock, he could pass for fifteen. He was wearing a black hoodie, jeans, and black Chucks. He sat down on a chair which was parked at the end of the couch.

"Hey Gill," said Lizzie.

"Lizzie."

"You got a light dude?" asked Brock.

Gill reached down and unzipped a black leather fanny pack which hung around his waist. They'd been out of style for over a decade, but Gill loved its practicality and almost always wore one. "Here you go." He tossed Brock a lighter.

They finished the joint off and Brock noticed Gill had an unusually silly ass grin on his face. "Dude. What's going on?"

Gill looked up at Brock, shook his head up and down, his grin broadened. "I found our way in, man."

"No shit."

"No shit, dude."

"How?"

"Not how," said Gill, "Who. but I'll fill you in later."

"What are you guys talking about?" asked Lizzie.

"It's just an online game thing we've been trying to figure out," said Brock.

"Is it something to do with the new Left 4 Dead? I've been wanting to play it since it came out."

"No, it's more like our own project," said Brock. He stared across at Lizzie, the lust so strong in his chest it almost hurt. She was a gamer too.

Lizzie smiled back at Brock - a knowing smile. "I'll let you guys do your game thing, whatever it is. I've got homework to do. I'm like way behind."

"Dude," said Gill, "Let's fire up your box, we've got some shit to go over."

Brock got up and walked across to his make-shift desk, a big slab of plywood held up by two sawhorses. He reached under the desk and turned on his computer. Gill grabbed the second chair and pulled it up next to Brock. Lizzie stepped up behind him and watched the Computer screen come to life. The splash came up.

"Ubuntu," asked Lizzie, "What's that?"

"It's a Linux distro," replied Brock.

"A system far superior to the Windows OS," said Gill, smugly. "By the end of next year it will completely dominate the market."

"I'll leave you boys with your toys." She bent down and gave Brock a kiss. "Call me." Before Brock could answer, she was hopping up the steps and out the door.

"Speak to me Gill."

"Her name is Shelly Knoller. I found her profile on Facebook. It took me like two tries to figure out her password at ARIL."

"So, we're in?"

"Oh, we're in," said Gill, nodding again. "Our Miss Knoller is a department head, so we've got access to everything."

Now Brock grinned. "That rocks, man."

"Is your VPN on?"

"Is the priest a pedophile."

"Use a domestic gateway, as close to home as possible." said Gill, looking over Brock's shoulder. "A foreign IP address might trigger an alarm in their network."

"I'll use a Chicago server."

"You're not using the IPSec protocol anymore?" asked Gill.

"No man. I switched to OpenVPN over a year ago."

"Good man. Now, call up ARIL's website and go to their intranet login, the link's at the bottom of the page." Gill leaned in closer to the screen. "Cool. Username, shelly.knoller.CFO, password, steven, all lowercase."

Brock stopped and looked up at Gill. "Dude, no fucking way."

"Yep. I thought the same thing. I was crossing ARIL employees with Facebook profiles. Shelly Knoller, a single mother, her page covered in pics of her son, Steven. I tried Steven98, included his birth year, no go. Then I thought, what the fuck, tried steven, all lowercase, presto! The door opened."

"How could their network admins let that ride?"

"No idea. She's been with the company for a long time, she's the controller, practically running the business side of the operation, I guess nobody had the balls to confront her on it."

Brock typed in the password. "OK. I'm in. Unfuckingbelievable."

"Go to her user settings."

"All right."

"She's got super admin rights, meaning we have access to pretty much everything," said Gill. "Every employee password and user profile, the entire database, customers, inventory, all of it. We even have keypad pins to get in the fucking building. The internal locks are all old-school, but that won't be a problem. We'll be inside with the security system shut down."

"Dude. We can really do this," Brock smiled up at Gill.

"Fucking A. Now, log off, and let me use your computer," Gill pulled a USB flash drive out of his fanny pack and took Brock's place in front of the computer. "Last night I pulled everything I could get off their system and copied it straight to this USB drive, locked it up with TrueCrypt's new XTC 512 bit encryption."

"No backup?"

"We want nothing incriminating on our computers." Gill typed out a series of passwords to get access to all the files on the drive. "I also pulled some satellite pics from Google maps." He double clicked on a jpeg file and the image opened, the top of the building clearly seen from Google's satellite.

Brock leaned forward to get a better view of the image. "Looks a lot bigger from space than when driving by in front of it."

"They do that on purpose. It's all about keeping a low profile, attracting as little attention as possible. The front of the building looks like a small office building, could be anything, but the rear of the place is a huge windowless block backing up against the woods on the far of Washington Park. Take the name, ARIL, sounds like a fucking Disney movie, but look behind the acronym - Animal Research Industrial Labs, and you find a monster of a different color."

"And you already looked over their inventory," asked Brock.

Gill opened a second file and a long list came up. "What you'd expect from an animal research place, and a few odd things you wouldn't expect." He scrolled down the list. "They have livestock in there, even stranger, there's a listing for a Lewis, no animal breed or race, nothing, just Lewis?"

Brock frowned. "No fucking clue. I guess we'll see." He stood up straight. "I do think our little stunt will blow their low profile right to the headlines—all over the country. This is gonna be big, dude. When are we doing it?"

"I'd say we do it in the next few days. It could be one of their IT guys notices our snooping around on the system on the log files. The sooner the better." Gill closed the open files and pulled out the USB drive. "I need to read up on the best way to get through locked doors inside the building."

"What about the computers?"

"No problem. There are roughly sixty Windows clients, two Windows servers, and a half dozen Linux servers. I'll just need a few minutes to upload my script and execute it. By the time the first guy shows up for work the next day there won't be nothing left but a big pile of ones and zeros. It will bring those sick assholes down to their knees."

Blood, Guts and Feathers (Three Days Later)

Brock walking out of the radio station after work shot off a text to Lizzie.

Brock: *What are you doing tonight?*

Lizzie: *Shift ends at 7. Why?*

Brock: *Wanna go to a concert?*

Lizzie: *Where? Who's playing?*

Brock: *Moby Dick's. Blood, Guts and Feathers.*

Lizzie: *Was told MD closed down after shooting. Never heard of the band?*

Brock: *MD reopened a month ago. BG&F are a punk band, big in animal rights movement.*

Lizzie: *Sounds good. Where should we meet?*

Brock: *I'll pick you up at 8.*

Lizzie: *8:30.*

Brock: *OK*

Lizzie: *XXX*

"What did you think of the band?" Brock asked. They were walking down the street two blocks from Moby Dick's.

"They're very intense. Besides, I have to like them now, a cute guy bought me a t-shirt," said Lizzie, holding up her arm with the t-shirt folded over it.

"They've been on the front line of the animal rights movement for the last decade."

"Are they part of the whole PETA movement?" asked Lizzie.

Brock stopped and turned toward Lizzie. "PETA is to make rich liberals feel better. I respect their ideas and their goals, but the only real changes have come from organizations like The Animal Liberation Front."

"ALF, I've read about them, and it would be hard to miss their logo in your apartment. Are you a member?"

Brock started walking down the street again. "Gill and I created our own sub charter."

"And what change could just the two of you make? There's power in numbers."

"Wait. In a few days, there'll be a big change around here." Brock knew as soon as the words left his mouth he'd gone too far.

Lizzie looked up, a question mark visible in her expression. "What big change?"

Brock tried to back-step. "How long have you been a vegan?"

"I became a vegetarian when I was twelve, and vegan two years ago. What big change?" She asked, stepping in closer to Brock.

Loose Lips

It took Lizzie two joints and a round of sex to squeeze everything about the ARIL project from Brock.

"I don't know." Lizzie was sitting on the couch facing Brock. "This all sounds pretty crazy. What if the police show up? You get arrested, maybe even shot."

Brock shrugged. "If the cops show, we'll throw our hands in the air and give it up—get as much press out of it as we can."

Lizzie paused, looked into Brock's eyes. "If you know what's going on in there, why not get some people together and protest the place, call some press in?"

Brock stood, walked over to his desk, shuffled through some papers, and returned to the couch. "This is how we even know about the place." He handed her a photocopy of a newspaper article from the Ponopolis Daily. "This article is from six years ago."

She read the headline, Protest at ARIL. There

was a picture of a crowd of people standing in front of a building, some carrying signs with catchy slogans like: Don't act blindly, treat Animals kindly, and No excuse for animal abuse. There was a couple standing in front of the crowd. The woman held a megaphone up to her face. She scanned the article: ARIL, a private animal research company in Ponopolis. The company was contracted to do some testing, but the bulk of its business was breeding, buying and selling animals for research labs across the country. The activists were accusing the company of inhumane practices against animals and that animal testing itself was unethical.

She looked up at Brock, but said nothing.

"I ran across this while doing some research for an article I was working on," said Brock. "Beside being mentioned a few times in blogs, the company has been flying under the radar ever since."

Brock stood and began pacing in front of the coffee table. "I've been fighting for animal rights since I was fifteen. I've been to dozens of protest rallies and marches. I've blogged, spread the word on social media—five years, and honestly, I see little progress." He stopped pacing and looked down at Lizzie. "It's time to step up the game. These people are slaughtering and torturing animals for cosmetic and pharmaceutical companies. Most of the research is pointless, and science has created better testing, in vitro technologies. Studying cell cultures in a petri dish produces better results, animal testing is outdated and unnecessary but for companies like

ARIL it's just business, the bottom-fucking-line."

Brock was getting louder now. He began pacing again. "Some days I think about quitting, giving up, get on with my life, but could I live with myself, do I want to live with that person?" He turned and looked down at Lizzie. "Maybe, if I do this one big thing, maybe the nightmares will stop."

Lizzie set the article down on the coffee table, looked up at Brock. "I want in."

The Pact

"You pussywhipped dumb-ass..." Gill sat on the chair across from Brock, his face turning red. "We said from the beginning of this thing we would involve no one else, we would tell no one else and we would fall in our fucking graves before we'd tell anyone else. Or did you forget our pact?"

"Dude, man, I'm sorry. I didn't forget the pact, but that was over a year ago. I didn't have a girlfriend then, now I do. It's not easy keeping something this big from a girlfriend."

"Pussywhipped, totally fucking pussywhipped." Gill leaned back and folded his arms across his chest.

"Guys, I'm sitting right here." Lizzie sat on the other end of the couch.

"Dude. All I can do is say I'm sorry." Brock spoke directly to Gill. "If you want out, I'll understand."

Gill's head tilted to the side. "Right. You'll get the script on their main server and run it? Do you even know which terminal to access in there?"

"I'm not the master-hacker you are. But, I'm not a complete noob either, I could figure it out."

Gill leaned forward, turned and looked at Lizzie, turned back to Brock. "Fuck you, man!" Gill lifted his arm and pointed his finger at Lizzie. "She's not coming in the building."

"Again, I'm sitting right here," said Lizzie.

The Raid

Brock and Lizzie were hiding deep in the woods behind ARIL. They could just make out the fence running along the company's property line and the rear of the building. Gill was riding his bike around the neighborhood, occasionally passing by the front of the company. They wanted to be absolutely certain there were no employees left in the building.

"You know, setting free all these animals, some of them will die and some will get recaptured," said Lizzie.

Brock turned his stare away from his vigil of ARIL and looked at Lizzie. "I remember showing the article to Gill the first time, we were stoned, and the idea of breaking in here and setting the animals free started as a joke, but the more we joked about it, the more it became real. I've been thinking about this night for a year, and yes, I know, some animals won't survive, but is the fate that awaits them in there, or some other research lab better?" Brock sat down and leaned against the trunk of a large oak tree. "There is hope that the press we get will trigger a reaction and other organizations will start rescue projects, to recapture the animals and set them free in the wild, or some will be adopted as pets." Brock smiled. "I like to dream that some of them will make it on their own."

Someone was coming up behind them through the woods. The person stopped, a second later they heard a high-pitched whistle.

"Sssstt, over here dude," said Brock.

Gill walked up, using a small penlight to navigate the dark woods. "You guys see anything?"

"No. You?"

"No. Not a living soul. All the lights are out, too."

"This is the point of no return," said Brock. He looked from Gill's face to Lizzie's, both nodded their head in affirmation. "OK, then."

Brock unzipped the top of his backpack and handed out gloves and black ski masks. "Let's go."

Using small beamed penlights they made their way through the woods up to the back of the fence. Gill removed his backpack and took out a pair of bolt-cutters. "I sharpened these, they should bite right through this chain link." He handed them to Lizzie.

She began cutting through the fence starting near the ground. The first links were difficult to get through, but she found if she made a hard, fast pinch it was easier going. In a few minutes she had an upside down 'L' about four-feet high. Gill pushed his body through the hole bending the fences inward; Brock followed him through.

"OK. Good job," said Gill. "Get as much of the fencing down as possible, the more you get down the easier it will be for the animals to get through to the park. Remember." Gill looked first at Lizzie, then at Brock. "You hear any sirens, an alarm goes off, anything goes wrong, don't wait, get out of here any way you can, and we'll meet at the rendezvous."

"Got it," said Lizzie. "The patch of woods at the top of the big hill on the north side of the park."

Brock leaned back through the fence and kissed Lizzie on the lips. "Love you, babe."

"Love you, too."

Gill let out an audible sigh, "I can't believe I'm doing this."

Brock and Gill snuck around the corner up to the side door, off the lower parking lot. Using Knoller's pin they were inside the building in a few seconds. They worked their way back toward the rear loading dock. They opened the door into the first animal storage area and the smell hit them like an invisible fist. Brock's eyes watered up instantly from the strong acrid ammonia in the air.

"Holly fuck!" said Gill. "How can anyone work here?"

"No idea. I can barely see."

They went through several storage rooms. Some animals were waking up and started to complain about the late night intrusion.

"The place feels a lot bigger inside than it looks from outside," said Brock.

"No locked doors so far, that's cool. Hopefully, we'll just have the loading dock door to get through."

They found the loading area and the rear loading-dock door. The room was about eight-hundred square feet. It could be entered from several wide doors from the various storage areas opposite the loading dock. There were stacks of empty cages, workbenches, and a small forklift parked in the corner next to an elevator.

"I got this." Gill walked up to the double door. He removed the bump key, from his pocket. "I ordered this online. I practiced on several locks at home. The secret is getting the right amount of pressure on the driver pins." He slid the bump key into the lock without turning it. He took out a slim metal bar and slid it into the head of the bump key. "Now... watch this." Using the metal bar he turned the key smoothly in the lock. Nothing. "It usually takes a few tries," said Gill.

After six attempts Brock got bored and started

looking around the room. He smiled and walked over to the corner of the room. "Dude."

Gill was so immersed in his lock picking task he didn't hear Brock.

"Dude."

Gill spun around. "Wait. I almost got it." His eyes widened. Brock was sitting in the forklift which was now pointing toward the door about twenty feet away. "How did you get that started?"

"The key was in it," said Brock. "Now get out of the way." He drove the forklift straight into the door. The forks hit the door, the doors flew open making a loud pop as the lock and one hinge broke. He saw Lizzie dive into the high grass on the other side of the fence. He whistled and made a quick wave. Lizzie got the message, jumped back to her feet and went back to work on the chain link.

Gill shook his head, looking at the key in his hand. "That was thirty bucks I could have spent on weed." He slid the key and metal bar back into his pocket. "I'll start with the surveillance, find the main server, then I'll be back to help with the animals."

"See you in a few, brother."

The surveillance equipment was easy to find. It was in a small closet-like office next to the main entrance. There were four monitors mounted on the wall above the desk, each one split into six active views from the two dozen cameras. The exterior cameras were using infrared, he could plainly see the ghost-like image of Lizzie on the back fence. He pressed and held the main power switch on the computer under the desk. In five seconds all monitors blinked off. He got on the floor and popped off the side of the computer's case. In under two-minutes he had the drive out and slipped it into his backpack. He left the small security office and went off in search of a terminal where he could access the company's main servers.

Brock started wandering through the animal storage areas and flipping on light switches. The largest room was to the right of the loading dock area. It contained hundreds of cages on shelves that stood eight feet above the floor. The cages contained thousands of rodents, mostly mice and rats. They were scuttling around after being hit by the bright fluorescent lights hanging from the ceiling.

Brock walked the length of the cages. He had never seen so many rodents all in one place. There were three large columns of cages filled with light brown rodents. He wasn't sure if they were big mice or small rats. He leaned forward, the label on the cages read Syrian Hamster. The next cages were filled with hundreds of rabbits, various breeds in a wide range of colors and shades. Some cages were packed so full, the rabbits were climbing all over each other, their fur matted and filthy. The smell was horrendous. Anything's better than this, Brock said to himself. He took a small digital camera out of his pocket and hung it around his neck. He took several pictures of the worst cages.

The next room was long and narrow. A shower curtain-like divider hung in the middle separating the canines on the right and the felines on the left. The room erupted in barks, growls and howls as soon as Brock flicked the lights on. He took a few steps along the cat aisle and stopped a few cages in. He looked into a cage on the second row. A large thin tabby lay on its side, it was wearing a plastic cone around its neck. It looked up at Brock, its eyes were red and swollen, crusted in a yellow puss. Brock took a picture, wiped the wetness from his eyes and continued down the aisle.

He opened the door to the last area; the smell was even worse, but less acrid somehow. It contained livestock. There was a pin with about a dozen small pigs. On the other side there were four stalls containing one cow each. He stepped up closer to the first stall; the cow turned its head and quietly looked at Brock. Something caught his eye, he stepped toward the rear of the animal. There was a large round disk protruding from the side of the cow, a large brown plug was stuck into the center of the disk. He leaned in closer; the disk was literally sewn into the side of the cow. Brock took three steps away from the stall, leaned forward and vomited into the straw and manure bits scattered on the floor.

He walked back toward the stall, there was a short leather rein wrapped over the top of the gate.

He struggled to open the clasp on the gate and slammed his palm into the side of the clasp. The metal stung, he stepped back from the gate and held his wrist waiting for the pain to reside. He stood straight, took a deep breath, pulled open the clasp, and opened the gate. Brock gently attached the rein to the cow's bridle and slowly started to walk back toward the loading area.

Brock and the cow strolled into the loading dock area. The cow lifted her head toward the open doors and sucked air deep into her lungs. "That smells good, doesn't it?" Brock reached forward and unclipped the rein. He tilted his head toward the open doors. "Madam, the night awaits."

The cow needed no more persuasion. She walked straight out the door, Brock heard her hooves speed up to a trot as she took off down the loading ramp. Two seconds later he heard, What the fuck? from out back. He stepped toward the door, "Sorry, should have warned you." By the time he was out on the ramp the cow had already passed through the fence and was trampling through the woods. Lizzie had already cut two long fifteen-foot holes through the fence.

She looked up at him. She was leaning against a fence post, one hand over her chest. "That scared the shit out of me."

"Sorry."

Lizzie tossed the bolt cutter on the ground. "That'll have to do. I don't think I have a cut left in me, my arms are exhausted." She walked over the grass and crossed the pavement.

"Perhaps," said Brock, "you should stay out here and keep a lookout."

She looked up at him. "Oh, shut up."

"Well, tell Gill I put up a fight."

They began exploring left of the loading dock. The first room was a large storage area containing pallets of animal feed, lab equipment, and even office supplies.

"Where are the labs?" asked Lizzie.

"I think they're one floor up. There's an elevator out there, it's probably used to take animals up and down."

When they opened the next door, the night burst into high-pitched screams and wails. Brock turned on the light. There were stacks of cages, three high, filled with monkeys. As they walked along the rows of cages, the monkeys screamed in protest. Some tried to reach out and grab at them; one threw excrement. The cages were labeled, most of the monkeys were macaques, there were some spider monkeys and even a few squirrel monkeys.

"I'm almost afraid to open up all the cages and set them free, some look aggressive, what if they attack us?"

"Nah," said Brock. "I don't think so. They can smell the night air out there. They'll take off for the park as soon as we open the doors. But let's look around, see what we're dealing with before we start opening cages."

"Yeah. like the cow?"

Brock stopped, wiped the sweat off his forehead. "She was an exception."

They opened the next door slowly, but heard nothing. Brock reached in and flicked the light on. It was a smaller room with a single large cage on the right. The cage was about ten-feet long and five deep. A single man-sized gorilla sat on a chair of two old car tires.

"That's a fucking gorilla!" said Lizzie.

Brock said nothing. He walked up closer to the cage; the cage's label read, Lewis. The gorilla didn't move, just sat on his tires and looked up at the intruders with tired red eyes. The floor of the cage was littered with fruit scraps and gorilla feces. "I hate this place. It's evil." Brock turned to look at Lizzie. "What kind of person could work here every day?"

"We can't let this one free," said Lizzie.

"I know." Brock walked across the room to the opposite door. The gorilla's eyes slowly followed him. He tried the knob, but it was locked. He turned to look back at Lizzie but they heard steps coming from the loading dock. There was no place to hide in the little room.

Gill burst into the room, but stopped running as soon as he saw them. He was panting, "Here you guys are."

"Fuck! Why are you running?" Brock's heart was still pounding in his chest.

"I was freaking out, I couldn't find anybody." Gill jumped back two steps. "Holy fuck! Is that a gorilla?"

"Gill meet Lewis, Lewis, Gill." Brock waved his hand back-and-forth making introductions.

"That's one mystery solved," said Gill

"This door's locked," said Brock, pointing at the guilty door.

Gill reached into his pocket and pulled out his bump key. "I knew this was a good investment."

On Gill's fifth try there was an audible click, and the door swung open. The room was silent, but the stench was even fouler than it had been in the previous rooms.

Gill reached in and turned the light on. He leaned forward and stuck his head in the door, looked back and forth once, pulled his head back and closed the door. "There aren't any animals we can free in there."

"Dude, what's in there?"

Gill looked at his friend in the face. "Death. Death is in there. Some kind of crematorium. It's not gonna help anyone to look in there. Besides, we gotta do this and get the hell out of here. We've already been here too long."

They started with the rodent area, then the livestock, and finished with the monkeys. They made a chain, Brock opened the cages and tapping a broom on the floor tried to herd them all toward the door. Gill stayed in the docking area, waving and slapping cardboard boxes together; but Brock had been right. They didn't need a lot of encouragement to flee. They could sense the night air and instinctively headed for the double door and out the back of the building. Lizzie was outside and using cardboard boxes also tried to direct them through the holes in the fence. Her job was harder, once outside the animals shot off in all directions. Most of the monkeys took off for the trees and never looked back.

After Brock finished opening all the cages in the monkey room, he stepped one last time into the gorilla's room. The beast still hadn't moved and sat peacefully on his tires looking up at Brock. "I really wish I could take you out of here, bring you to the biggest jungle in Africa." Brock paused. "Where you'd never have to see a fucking human again." He snapped a picture, turned and left the room.

Gill was still in the docking area fighting to herd rodents toward the door, an almost futile task. It was getting loud; dogs were barking, monkeys were screaming, and a whole chorus of other animal sounds.

"Let's get out of here," said Gill

Outside was no better, there were animals everywhere. A small pig was running back and forth along the fence line at an incredible speed. Brock's face was pinched in anxiety.

"Dude, we knew this wouldn't be a perfect escape."

"I know," said Brock.

The three of them took off into the woods and were quickly swallowed up into the dark.

The Vegas Job
Part IV

Dan stepped over to the window when he heard barking down the road. He had four dogs, a lab, two shepherds, and a pit bull—Johnny, Waylon, Willie, and Kris, named after the members of the supergroup, The Highwaymen. The dogs raised a ruckus over anyone coming down the drive who wasn't Lori or Doug.

He stood holding his cup of coffee and waited to see who was pulling in. He watched the black Mountaineer come up toward the house, Johnny and Kris trotting along on the driver's side, Willie and Waylon on the passenger side. The Mercury parked in front of the house about twenty feet from Doug's Jeep. The Dogs had the SUV surrounded, Jake and Fury knew enough not to get out of the car.

Dan walked to the front door and stepped out onto the porch. He stuck the tips of his index finger and thumb in his mouth and blew a sharp, high-pitched whistle. All four dogs broke formation and took off around the side of the ranch house to whereabouts unknown.

44 Hours Ago

I sat in the back of the van between several suitcases, still ruffled from being thrown and slugged around like a two-fingered-Keytarist. I knew Vegas well enough to know we were heading south out of town. I didn't know what to think of my two escorts; they claimed to be working for the twins. It was obvious they were working for somebody? I looked around the back of the van for anything I might be able to use for a weapon—just three suitcases. I'd play along, keeping my eyes open. "So... Jake, was it? Where are we headed?"

Without looking back, Jake said, "We were told to bring you to the ranch."

"OK. Where's the ranch? And will we hook up with Ray and the band there?"

Again, without looking back. "Colorado. Sorry. All I know is the band is camped out in the desert somewhere."

"Colorado? As far as I remember, Colorado's the other direction?"

This time Jake turned and looked back at me. He smiled and said. "We've got to shake Fabian's goons. They're still tailing us. And the plan is, they keep following us till Searchlight."

I started to turn my head to look out the rear window of the van.

"DON'T look back, man." said Jake, the smile still

holding to his face. "It's a better play, if they don't suspect we know they're back there."

"Got it." I said. "What's Searchlight?"

"Small town, about an hour south of Vegas, run by the Vegos, an old biker club that's been running South Nevada for a long time."

"So, you guys are with the Vegos?"

Fury laughed, which was the first sound he'd made.

"No we aren't with the Vegos. Listen, I know you're just trying to piece shit together, but we were paid to get you out of Vegas, bring you to the ranch. Best to save the questions for later."

"I think they're turning off." said Fury from behind the wheel. His voice was high and nasal, which didn't fit his large body and head.

"Perfect." said Jake. "Let's shed the patches before driving through Searchlight. Wouldn't be cool if the wrong eyes saw us wearing these vests."

"Definitely not." said Fury. "Hold the wheel, man."

Jake held the wheel and Fury stripped off the vest and tossed it on the floor behind his seat. Jake took his off too, and threw it on the floor next to Fury's.

We arrived in Flagstaff Arizona in the late evening. Fury pulled off the historical Route 66 and drove into the parking lot of a Super 8 hotel.

Fury turned to Jake. "You guys grab the bags and take them up to the rooms. I'll take care of the van."

Jake got out of the van and slid open the side door. "You heard him."

We carried the bags up to the second level, Jake pulled out a room key and opened the door. Although, the room had been cleaned, and the beds made, there were personal belongings lying around creating the impression that they'd been staying here for at least a few days.

"You got the adjoining room." He stepped up to me, his eyes made a quick scan from my feet up to my face. "Not going to be a tailor fit, but I'll lend you something to wear, you can take a shower, put on something clean."

I truly didn't know how to respond to that, I said, "Thanks man."

"Go shower, I'll lay something out on your bed."

My mindset on Jake and Fury was beginning to shift. I walked into the adjoining room. It looked like any budget hotel room you'd find along any American highway: two queen-sized beds, two generic landscape prints bolted to the wall, a dresser-drawer topped with a small flat-screen TV, a small bathroom opposite the front door. Their room was a few square inches bigger and had one king-sized bed.

I took a long hot shower, washed the three days of jail off my body. When I walked out of the bathroom, Jake had laid a complete outfit on the bed. Somehow I was expecting an old pair of Wrangler jeans and a Grateful Dead t-shirt, but instead, found a pair of designer jeans from All Mankind, a navy-blue blazer from T. Hilfiger, and a light blue dress shirt. He even added a pair of boxers and black silky socks. I was curious how the ensemble would pair with the old Chucks I'd been wearing when the police picked me up.

After dressing, I looked at myself in the large mirror above the dress-drawer. I didn't look this sharp at my cousin's wedding last year. I knocked on their door. Jake opened it, the transition was incredible. He was clad in white summer pants and a shiny black blazer. His long wavy hair was lightly oiled, pulled back over his head with a slight part on the side. The facial tattoos, including the teardrop under his eye, were gone. He could play lead in any daytime soap opera.

He stepped up to me and straightened the shoulders of my blazer. "Fits even better than I thought it would, jeans are a perfect fit." He frowned when he saw the old Chucks at the bottom of his stylish outfit. "What size shoe do you wear?"

"Eleven."

"Too bad. I'm a size bigger. Fury's still in the bathroom." Even his voice had a smoother feel to it.

"When you guys play a part, you play the part." I said.

Jake smiled. "As soon as he's ready, we'll get some dinner. Do you like Indian food? There's a decent Indian restaurant right across the highway. We'll eat, get a few hours of sleep, and then head up to the ranch, there's still a good seven hundred miles of road to cover."

I walked down to the reception. There was a pay phone on the outside wall next to an ice machine. I tried to call Ray, but was told by a friendly robot voice that the number was unavailable.

Jake was right, the food at the Indian place was decent. I had the Butter Chicken Curry. The biker personas were completely gone; when Fury stepped out his hotel room, he looked like a Texas banker. He wore a slick three-piece suit, a Bolo tie hung neatly around his neck, the dark leather aiguillette ran through a silver ornamental clasp, a snake wound around a pin, its two shiny turquoise eyes glistening in the light.

After a few rounds of beer and some Indian plum schnapps that Jake kept ordering, we laughed, traded a few stories, and the strain of the last three days eased away. It was obvious now; they were a couple and seemed to be a happy pair. I wondered what it'd be like to travel around doing gangster shit with your better half. I laughed at myself, how different was that from traveling around with a band doing gangster shit. I laughed a second time; I've been walking around telling everyone I'm a musician for so long, I believe it myself.

"What's so funny?" asked Jake.

I smiled, it was the most genuine smile I'd had in a few days. "Life, man. Life is a goddamn, funny thing."

"I'll drink to that." Fury held his drink up high, and we toasted.

"I gotta ask, why the fuck were you guys in jail?"

"Twins thought Fabian's guys might try to jack you up on the inside, we were there for backup," said Jake.

"And you just go in and out of the jail whenever you feel like it?"

Fury leaned in. "Vegas is our city man, that's why we get paid the big bucks." They both laughed.

The next morning they checked out of the hotel rooms and we carried the bags to a black Mercury Mountaineer. "What happened to the van?" I asked.

"What van?" said Fury.

I shrugged and climbed into the back seat; a lot more comfortable than sitting on the floor in the back of a van. Fury drove again, Jake rode shotgun. It was dry barren landscape, and it felt good to sit back and watch it roll by, and my travel companions had a good taste in highway music.

The Ranch

We parked in front of the ranch house; the SUV surrounded by four large, and angry looking dogs. A man, who looked familiar, stepped out on the porch and whistled. All four dogs simultaneously stopped growling and smacking their jaws and took off around the house together. We all three got out of the car and walked up the steps to the porch. The man who greeted us was wearing a bathrobe and a Stetson. I stared at his face trying to place where I'd seen him before.

He smiled, a big cowboy smile. "Billy. We meet again."

And like the snap of a twig, as soon as he spoke, I remembered where I knew him from; Moby Dick's, the night of the shooting. And more cards started falling into place. He's an old friend of Ray's, the ranch, he must be one of the twins? "Dan?" I said.

"That's my name." He held his hand out.

I shook his hand.

"Jake, Fury. Welcome." After a quick round of handshakes and shoulder pats he invited everyone inside.

We sat at a long solid oak table in leather-upholstered chairs. Dan brought in a round of coffee.

"Ray and the band?" I asked.

"I've been on the horn with him all week. Don't fret none, I'll fill you in on all that real soon."

Another guy who I don't remember seeing before came down from upstairs. He got a cup of coffee and sat down—a good half-foot shorter than Dan, a resemblance was there, same dusty blond hair, same eyes.

"This here's my brother, Doug. Doug, this here's Billy, the bass player with Ray's band."

"Nice to meet you." I said.

"Likewise." He took a drink from his cup.

After a quick breakfast of pancakes and sausages Jake and Fury said they had to get back to Vegas, monitor the situation there.

I was on my fourth cup of coffee, Doug had barely said anything. From time to time I'd caught him staring at me.

Dan came back into the dining room from the kitchen. "Sorry, that breakfast was as bland as Arizona sand. If Lori was here, she'd have fixed up something a lot more exciting."

"Lori. I remember her. She was there, too, at Moby Dick's? She broke her ankle?"

"Well," said Dan, sitting down at the end of the table. "Fortunately, it wasn't broken, just a sprain. She got caught in the stampede when that bat-shit weasel started shooting the place up. She's fine now."

"What happened to the rifle?" asked Doug.

"No idea," said Dan. "Guess the cops got it."

"They say it was a classic Henry in mint condition. That'd be a perfect fit in my collection."

Dan stared across at his brother, but said nothing. Finally he turned to me, smiled, and asked. "Billy bass player, you know how to ride a horse?"

Dan rode a big shiny dark brown stallion, he tried to bite me when I got too close. Dan gave me a much smaller gelding after I confessed that I'd only ridden a horse twice when I was fifteen. He was a plump, friendly old horse with a reddish grey coat. Dan told me his name was Mickie, but the few times I called his name he gave no indication that he knew it, and just plodded along next to Dan's horse.

We rode along over the dry hills. Dan showed me his ranch, or spread, as he called it.

Dan pulled up lightly on the rein and stopped at the top of the ridge. My horse obediently copied Dan's horse and pulled up next to them.

"My brother doesn't like it down here; says it's too hot and dry. But look at this view. I love the openness, I feel free down here."

"The view is something." I couldn't come up with anything better.

He turned and looked me in the eyes. "I apologize for the bad intel, Billy. Our source should have known about that extra alarm on the guitar." He looked away, back over the hills.

"Well," I said. "Can't draw a flush every hand."

He laughed. His big cowboy smile returned to his face. "Billy-boy, I think some of that Vegas jail rubbed off on you."

"Why steal a guitar like that? So, some other rich dude can hang it up in his basement? It's a one-of-a-kind."

Dan turned back to me. "No." He shook his head. "Nothing like that." He spit on the ground. "It's politics. Just politics." He paused. "What do you know about the Chicago outfit?"

I looked at him, but said nothing.

"Except for the five families of New York, the Chicago outfit is one of the biggest syndicates in the US. They started taking an interest in Vegas back in the forties and were behind a lot of the big casinos being built back then. After a lot of internal fighting in the outfit, and pressure from the FBI, they lost control of Vegas. It started getting taken over by big corporations, but now it's a new century, the outfit is tight again, and they want their desert gem back."

"And the guitar?" I shrugged.

"Fabian's a medium-sized player in Vegas, and independent; took over the operation his father started in the early seventies. He's been at odds, off and on, for years with the Vegos, a biker club that's been running everything south of Vegas for decades. The old divide and conquer, works every time—start a little war between Fabian and the bikers, step in, bring back order, and start taking over."

I felt a rot in my gut. I thought we were being paid to steal something that somebody else wanted; not start a fucking mob war in Las Vegas.

Dan looked at me, a sympathetic smile on his face. "Billy, man, that's politics. If they hadn't hired us, they'd have hired some other sidewinders."

"But the plan didn't work. I got picked up by the cops."

"I'll admit, plan A, went a little south, but plan B seems to be holding together."

"Plan B?"

"I'll let Ray fill you in on that, He made most of it happen, anyway. We should get back. I got some calls to make." He spun his horse around and started back down the ridge.

Mickie, ignoring me, followed.

"I'd like to talk to Ray."

"He's expecting your call, but call him between five and six o'clock. There's no reception where they're staying, so he drives into town once a day. You can reach him then."

"Where are they?"

"As of yesterday, they were holding up at some campground outside of Vegas. We'd have taken you there, but we didn't want to risk it. I wanted to get you as far from Vegas as possible."

"So, the plan is, they pick me up on their way back to Ponopolis?" I asked.

"Not necessary. Doug's heading back to Ponopolis in the morning. He'll take you."

I nodded.

Back at the Ranch I called Ray:

"Yeah."

"This is B."

"Good to hear your voice brother."

"Good to be heard."

"Where're you guys at?"

"Campground, over the Arizona border. You?"

"At the ranch."

"Need a ride back home?"

"No. Doug's heading up to Ponopolis in the morning. I'll catch a ride with him."

"Sounds good. We'll break camp here, should be back home sometime late Thursday."

"Cool. I'm looking forward to seeing you guys."

"All right. Let's get this shit behind us and start recording. We were sitting around a campfire last night, worked on some new material."

"Can't wait."

Dan burned up a few rib-eye steaks and served them with deli potato salad and a can of baked beans. He apologized, once again, for his lack of finesse in the kitchen and how much he missed Lori's cooking.

After dinner we sat in front of a fire in the den, drank whiskey. The whiskey was mellow and tasted like old smoke; it was the best liquor I'd ever remembered drinking. Dan did most of the speaking and seemed happy to do so. Doug didn't talk a lot. Again, I caught him giving me eerie side glances, or was it just the way the light and shadows from the fire danced off the side of his face? Dan asked me how the new material was coming along for the upcoming recordings. He spoke about the time they were teenagers in Northern Minnesota and when they'd first met Ray; it was some place called Two Harbors. The way Dan told the story was hilarious, and it had us all laughing, even Doug.

"SSsst... Hey, Billy. Gotta wake up."

I rolled over on the bed and looked up, Doug's face slowly came into focus. My head felt like someone had replaced half the brain matter with cotton. I'm guessing I'd overdone it on the whiskey last night.

"You need to get up now." Doug said. He was already dressed and had a clean shave.

"What time is it?" I asked.

"Almost five. I'd like to get an early start; beat the traffic." He turned and headed back out of the room. "I'll wait downstairs. Let's hit the road in fifteen."

I sat up, maybe too quickly, the cotton in my head didn't like it. What traffic are we going to beat, I thought? We were in the middle of nowhere in Western Colorado.

I splashed some water on my face, got dressed, and went downstairs.

Doug was sitting on a bar stool at the kitchen counter. There were two tall travel mugs on the counter in front of him.

"I made us some coffee for the road."

Dan woke up two hours later. The door to Doug's bedroom was standing open. He smiled, the bed was neatly made, and the room tidied up; his brother, if anything, was disciplined.

In the kitchen he saw there was still some coffee left in the bottom of the pot. He felt it with his finger, still lukewarm—good enough. He filled up a coffee mug and walked to the front porch.

He sat in his rocker, looked out over the valley and drank his coffee. Some clouds were moving in from the west, some rain would be good, it's been dry. Something was gnawing at his brain. It wasn't unusual for his brother to get up early and take off, Doug rarely slept past six. What was unusual was that he had volunteered to take the bass player back to Ponopolis? Sure, he lived on the family farm an hour from the city, but his brother had always been a loner and Dan couldn't imagine he'd enjoy the company of a stranger on a road trip half-way across the country. If asked, he could be very generous, but he wasn't a volunteer type of guy.

Dan reached up and scratched his head. There was something more, and he was racking his brain trying to find it. Dan stood up, "Ah fuck." he mumbled to himself. He walked back into the house, he'd need to be fast.

Ten minutes later, he was dressed and rolling his bike, a green Kawasaki ZX-10R, out of the barn. It'd be a long ride, but he'd make better time on it.

Doug stayed on smaller county highways to avoid getting too close to Denver. It took us a good part of the day, but we finally reached Interstate 80. Unlike Jake and Fury, Doug was a quiet travel companion. It was several hours of landscape and classic rock music before Doug looked over at me and asked, "You hungry?"

I still had a decent hangover, and I was starving, but I replied with a curt, "Yeah."

After burning up over twelve hours of road, Doug pulled into a rest area. "My eyes need a break. Can you take over on the wheel for a few hours?"

"No problem."

I got out, stretched my back, and walked around to the driver's side. I smiled over at Doug. "You know, I don't think I've ever driven a Jeep before."

"You fuck up my Jeep, I'll kill you." Doug grinned at me; a wide toothy grin.

I drove down the highway, Doug lowered the back of his seat and closed his eyes. I wasn't a hundred percent sure if he slept, or just had his eyes closed, but he didn't make a sound.

It was a boring stretch of highway, straight, flat, corn on the right, corn on the left, and occasionally, I'd get a farmhouse to look at, like little islands on a giant sea of corn. I wondered what it must be like to live like that. My mind started building the whole scenario; sitting at a Formica table in an old farm kitchen. wearing worn-out overalls, my wife in a loose flowery pastel dress cooking breakfast—I don't know where the kids were, probably hiding behind the barn smoking.

Suddenly, without warning, Doug sat up from his seat, a burst of air exploding from his lungs, his eyes wide open. I was so startled; the Jeep swerved slightly onto the shoulder. He looked at me. "Where are we?"

"Still on the same highway you told me to stay on." I said.

Doug took over driving for the last stretch of road. "A few more hours, we'll be home."

"Where the buffalo roam," I added.

"Our family farm is right on the way; about an hour south of Ponopolis. We need to make a quick stop there, and then I'll take you up to the city."

"Cool. Could you could drop me off at the warehouse? My bike's there."

"Is it a domestic, or a Jap bike like Dan farts around on?"

"It's just on an old bicycle. I have no idea where it was made."

Doug looked over at me. "You ride a bicycle? You're a grown man. You don't have a car or a motorcycle, or something?"

"Nah man. I live in the city. It's all I need."

"I can't believe I let you drive my Jeep."

We pulled off the county road onto a long gravel drive, wound through about a half-mile of dense woods, crossed over a small bridge. "Witkotkoke Creek," Doug informed me, all the consonants in the name stuck in his throat.

I looked over the edge of the bridge into the narrow creek, but a second later my eyes were drawn up. Past the bridge the road sloped up a steep hill. A massive house that must have been over a hundred years old was perched majestically at the top of the hill.

"Our great grandpa built the original house in eighteen-ninety."

As the car drew up the hill and circled around to the back, I could see that several additions had been built off the original house, more than doubling its size. There was a big barn, two sheds, and what looked like had once been a chicken coup in the back. "It's big." I said. Turning back to the house "How many people live here?"

"It's just me now. Our folks passed away a few years back. We got two older brothers, but they moved away years ago. One's out in California, the other is in Sweden."

"So you live in this big house alone?"

"Yep."

"Must get lonely, man."

Doug parked the Jeep behind the house, looked at me with his dead-pan expression. "I could leave my family home, move to the city," he said. "Pedal a fucking bicycle around."

He grabbed a duffle bag out of the Jeep, opened the door and went in. I was a light traveler, only the borrowed-outfit from Jake I was wearing, my wallet, keyring, and some pocket change. My phone and luggage were in the Dread Sled.

Doug threw his bag on the floor in the hall next to the kitchen. Inside, it smelled like a house that four generations had lived in, each one leaving behind their own scent in the wood and plaster. The house was a time-machine, some furniture went back decades, while other pieces were relatively new. The bric-à-brac too; I saw a tin model racing car on the mantel that was at least sixty years old, next to a seventies era lava lamp.

Doug walked into the kitchen, opened the refrigerator door. "I'm fucking starving. Let's see what we got." He started tossing stuff onto the kitchen counter. "A sandwich? I'll make us some sandwiches."

I was hungry, but I wanted to go home. I wanted to strip off Jake's clothes which I'd been wearing for a few days now, shower, and crash in my own bed, in my own apartment. It felt strange being around either of the twins. They had been my mystery bosses for a long time. I had never met them. I never knew their names. And now, in the last forty-eight hours, I'd been to both their houses, drinking, eating, and shooting-the-shit with them like we were old pals. So I sat down at the table and replied. "A sandwich sounds good. Thanks, dude."

In a few minutes he constructed two sandwiches which seemed to include some kind of meat, cheese, lettuce and mayo. "There you go." he set the plate on the table and slid it over to me. He went back into the refrigerator. "Cool. Billy you gotta try this. My family's been making this tea for about a hundred years—it's fucking great." He pulled out a big gallon jug that was half-full of a hazel brown liquid. "Sassafras tea." he proclaimed. "It's made from tree root."

I'd never heard of the stuff. I just stared at the jug and nodded my head.

"It's better with a slice of orange." He turned back to the counter, sliced up an orange, dropped some ice cubes into two pint-sized glasses, poured the brown liquid over it, slid one glass over to me, and sat down.

I took a bite of the sandwich; it tasted like peppered roast beef. I didn't know what to make of the tea. It had a dark earthy aroma; it really wasn't bad.

"Billy." Doug said, after swallowing the last bite of his sandwich. "I'd just like to say thanks." He smiled.

"OK. What for?" I nodded.

"You've been with Ray's crew for a while now.

Except for this Vegas fuck-up, you guys have done a great job, we've all been making some money, and I thought, now would be a good time to say so."

I was about to bring up the bad intel we had on the job, but decided not to. I replied. "Thanks. We appreciated the work, and the money." A small chuckle muffled out of my mouth.

Doug tried to chuckle, but it came out more like three short chokes. "I like Ray," he said. "And it was nice meeting you."

"Likewise," I said. His small round face suddenly grew smaller. The kitchen behind him seemed to blow out about ten feet and abruptly suck back in even closer. My upper body started tipping forward, and my spine didn't want to help stop it. I slammed both hands on the table in front of me to stop from falling forward. It worked for a second. I looked up at Doug.

He was still smiling, "Nothing personal, Billy. It's just business."

That's all I remember.

The Hill

An agonizing roar was growing louder and louder; I reached up and pressed on the sides of my skull to hold it together. I tried to open my eyes, but the light increased the pain in my skull. The screeching noise grew louder, I tried wrapping my arms around my head to dampen the sound. All at once, the awful noise stopped, leaving a hollow ringing in my head. I started to sit up; but my wrists were tied?

"Billy?"

I turned my head toward the sound.

"Billy, you all right?"

I forced my eyes open, the light shot through my skull, it hurt, but after an agonizing amount of time, Dan's face came into focus. "Dan?" My foggy mind was trying to piece things together. I looked to the right, the left, I looked down. I was sitting in a small trailer which was parked on a hill. There were trees, the leaves gold and brown. I looked back up at Dan. "What the fuck."

"Big Dan, to the rescue." Doug walked out between some trees toward us. He was carrying a shovel.

"Doug. What the fuck, man?" Dan turned and faced his brother.

"Tying up loose ends, brother, doing the work you wouldn't do."

"Were you back there digging a hole?"

"Like I said, loose ends." The volume of Doug's voice went up a notch which stung the back of my brain, but my head was clearing.

"What the fuck is your problem?"

Doug smiled, looked at his brother in the eyes. "He wouldn't be alone up here, brother, would he? No... He'd have lots of company on this hill."

"Dude! What loose ends?" Dan's voice went up to match his brother's volume. "Fabian decimated the Vegos, but his organization was left bleeding. The last thing anybody in Vegas is thinking about is a lone bass player walking around after a concert. The plan worked like a charm. Chicago couldn't be happier."

"Fabian's no dipshit. When all this shit settles, he's gonna start looking for clues. He's gonna want to know what happened to that bass player." The volume in Doug's voice went back down, but it remained tense.

"No. Fabian isn't a dipshit. But Fabian already has a meeting set up with Chicago," condescension leaking into Dan's voice. "And before he can say, aces-over-eights, the outfit will be all but running the place—and those boys have got our back. We're out of the woods, brother." Dan stepped in closer to his brother. "But let's be honest, this ain't really about no *loose end*, is it, brother? No. This is about something that happened a long time ago. This is about Priscilla."

"What the fuck are you talking about?" Doug's voice got louder again, but it didn't sting as much, everything was coming back.

The job, jail, the road trip with Jake and Fury, the ranch, the twins, and now, sitting here in the back of this trailer on a hill in the middle of the woods. The trailer was attached to a four-wheeler. I could see a big green motorcycle parked on a dirt trial which wound through a small field and around the bottom of the hill.

"Ever since that chick dumped you and hooked up with that drummer. What was his name? Mark?"

"Fuck you. This is business." Doug's face was red, now. He started stammering.

"The other night, we were all sitting around, drinking, talking. You joked; *Can't trust musicians, they're all a bunch of low-life fuck-ups.*" Dan pulled a buck knife out of a sheath on his belt. "I saw the look on your face, and I've known you since I was five minutes old. The next morning, I knew what you were planning. You've hated musicians since Priscilla, that's why you've always hated Ray." He turned around and faced me, bent down, grabbed the rope that was binding my wrists, pulled it up, and deftly cut through it in one slice. He looked down, gave me his humble cowboy smile.

WHAAMM!

Dan dropped like a bass drum, but quieter. Doug was standing behind him, he was holding the shovel up. His face was dark red, his eyes glowed in anger.

"Fuck you, big brother." He looked up at me, one hand slowly reaching behind his back.

I quickly spun around and jumped out of the trailer and down behind the opposite side between the trailer and the four-wheeler. I heard the distinctive metal click of a hammer being cocked.

"Billy bass player, why don't you come out of there now?" There was a sinister oil in his voice.

I pictured him standing at the opposite end of the trailer, a pistol raised and pointing just above the rim of the trailer wall. I pulled the hitch pin from the trailer hitch, slow and quietly as I could, I lifted the coupler off the ball. I wrapped my arm around the trailer tongue, dug both feet in, and pushed up and forward as hard as I could.

I heard a short yelp from Doug. He hadn't had time to get out of the way and the trailer rolled over him; Something snapped, it could have been a branch, I was hoping it was bone.

I circled around to the right. BAM! He shot off the gun. He was somewhere under the trailer. He was probably shooting at my feet. I ran as fast as I could down the hill, taking big high leaps. BAM! A second shot.

I flipped up the kickstand and jumped on the back of the big green motorcycle. The key was in the ignition. I started it up, pulled in the clutch, and started going through the gears with my foot. I hadn't ridden a motorcycle in years, and never a big fancy thing like this. BAM! I ducked my head lower.

I let out the clutch and hit the throttle. The bike lurched out about three feet and slammed to a halt. "Shit!" I yelled. I tried it again, a little smoother. The motorcycle took off down the path like a motherfucker. BAM! Fuck him, I had to be out of range. I didn't know where the trail led, but any place was better than here.

Uncle Al

After stashing the Ford Focus in Searchlight, Ray and Rip returned the tow-truck to Phoenix. They'd both had enough driving for one night and checked into a Motel Six off of highway sixty. They slept until noon and grabbed a late breakfast at the Denny's across the street.

It was still light out when they pulled into Lloyd's Campground. They parked Polly's truck next to her house and walked to site three.

Nobody was sitting around in front of the Dread Sled but something caught Ray's eye across the road. "What the fuck?"

Rip saw them too and laughed. "Well, they've been busy."

Mal, Ktel, and Polly were all at the small pool next to the campground's shower house and restrooms. The pool now seemed to be in working order and filled with water because Ktel had just done a cannonball into the deep end of it.

Ray, followed by Rip, walked over to the pool. Ray didn't say anything, He only smiled and watched his band.

Polly was sitting in a deck chair working on a glass of wine. Mal was lying next to the pool on a beach towel in a cute one-piece bathing suit, she was laughing and yelling at Ktel for getting her wet.

Mal looked up. "Hey guys."

"Ktel fixed the pool?" asked Rip.

"Ktel fixed the pump. Polly and me cleaned it all out," said Mal.

Polly held her hand above her eyes to block the setting sun. "It had been broken for ten years. Cesar tried to fix the damn thing a few times, we thought the thing was shot."

"Ktel can fix anything," said Mal.

"Not everything," said Ktel. "I ain't never been able to fix Ray's guitar solos."

"Ha ha ha, fuck you," said Ray. "I'm getting my swimming trunks, and there'd better be an adequate supply of beer in the camper, I ain't driving back to town."

It was a beautiful desert night. After eating Fajitas, and some of Polly's *world-famous guacamole*, they all sat around a campfire next to the camper.

Rip held up his beer. "To B. Wherever you are."

"To B," said everyone else in unison.

"I was working on a new song a few hours ago," said Ray.

"Are you talking about the two-note riff you were jamming earlier," asked Ktel.

Ray smiled at him, nodding his head. "I love you, man. I don't know how, or why, but I love you."

"Let's hear it," said Rip.

Ray walked into the camper and got his acoustic guitar, a Gibson Hummingbird, and a sheet of paper. "Still a few lines to smooth out in the lyrics." He sat down on a Coleman cooler with his guitar and placed the sheet on his knee.

"Does it got a title?" asked Mal.

Ray looked up at her. "It's called, *Uncle Al.*"

"Who the fuck is Uncle Al," asked Rip, grinning.

"He was my uncle."

"I've known you since the Iron Range, and you've never mentioned any uncle dude named Al," said Rip

"I never met the man. He lived in some hick town, called Seymour, down in Indiana." Ray started looking through his pockets while balancing the guitar and the sheet of paper. "He had a notorious reputation for being a bible smacking, redneck, pool hustler who hated any modern ideas. Anybody got a pick?" asked Ray.

"I got one," said Rip. He dug around in his front pocket, pulled out a guitar pick and handed it over to Ray.

Ray wondered why a drummer walked around with guitar picks in his pocket, but ignored it and went on with his story. "His name often came up at family get-togethers. Some people liked him, but my mom hated him."

"Your ma's so cute," said Mal.

Ray nodded on went on. "Anyway, I got an email two weeks ago that he died. I was jamming earlier, he drifted into my thoughts, and I wrote it down."

"Well, play it," said Rip.

"Now you gotta fucking play it," said Ktel.

"It starts with the chorus: *G7, B-flat, C-major.*"

"Play the song. We'll figure it out," said Mal. She sat up straight, laid both hands flat on the table in front of her. "My air piano's ready to roll. Rip?"

Rip grabbed two spoons off the table. "Check."

Ray strummed down heavy on the first chord and jumped into the intro. It was a rocking honky-tonk progression. Rip started tapping out the beat with the spoons on the tabletop, but quickly changed his mind, tossed the spoons aside, spun around, started thumping his feet on the ground to keep the beat, clapping his hands and banging on his knees. Mal's fingers looked for the chords on her air piano as she started humming the piano melody.

"Hey! Where's uncle Al!" Ray shouted. "Everybody!"

In unison they sang, *"Hey! Where's uncle Al!"*

Ray went down a notch. *"Guess he's hiding from you."*

"Hey! Where's uncle Al!" Shouted everybody.

Ray: *"Guess you don't have a clue—the verse."*

Ray brought the guitar down and went into a groovy western progression. Rip followed with his hands and knees, Mal on air piano.

Think he's hiding—down in that cellar room
Far far from—the likes of you
He just don't know—your kind of boogie
Don't know nothing new—don't have a clue
He'd rather slam—he'd rather jam
That old fool and his—old-school moves
Than dance with all them kids
Eccentric queens in their—electric shoes

"Now the riff," shouted Ray.

"*Ooowwwww,*" howled Ktel

The riff grooved in its simplicity. Polly's head was bobbing along, a wide bright smile ran across her face.

"Back to the chorus," sang Ray. He went back to the chorus, but fattened it up using power chords.

And they all sang: "*Hey! Where's Uncle Al!*"

They jammed on for a few more progressions.

"Let's wrap this up," said Ray. He dropped into a short rag-time progression—and stopped.

Everybody clapped and howled.

"That is a cool number, dude," said Ktel.

Polly was beaming. "This is the most fun I've had since the sixties."

Home Sweet Home

The next evening, Ray and Ktel drove into the campgrounds just past six o'clock. Mal was in the camper playing her fiddle and Rip was at the pool.

"Rip!" When Rip looked up, Ray gestured that he return to the camper. "Mal," He said into the camper.

When they were all together next to the Dread Sled, Ray began, "I just talked to Billy, he's at a ranch up in Colorado with the twins. It seems our plan worked, and nobody's looking for him."

"So, let's go pick him up," said Mal.

"No need. He'll catch a ride with one of the twins."

"Why are we still hanging around here?" asked Rip.

"We ain't," said Ray. "Let's get our shit together, point the Dread Sled northeast and go home."

"Home sweet home," said Mal.

Before hitting the road they all walked over to Polly's house together.

When she stepped out, Ray handed her an envelope. "This is for our site."

"I couldn't take money from y'all. No way." The

dismay in her expression was obvious as her eyes looked from one face to the next.

"You need it more than we do," said Ray. "Besides, you gotta keep this campground running so we have a place to stay on our southwest tours." He extended his hand putting the envelope inches in front of her.

She looked doubtful, but reached out and took it. Mal smiled and nodded at her. After hugs, and a few tears from Polly they jumped into the Dread Sled and took off for home.

Woodstock

Fabian Delbowski sat behind his desk, his chin propped up in his fist. His eyes staring across the room at nothing, when someone knocked on the door.

Fabian's eyes shifted toward the double doors, but he said nothing.

The door knob turned. Fabian flipped the safety off on the Desert Eagle which was resting on his knee in his right hand under the desk. Only three people in Fabian's circle would walk into his office uninvited. And one of those three was Lucas Bennett, his lawyer and long-time confidant, who stepped into the office, shut the door, and strolled over to his usual place next to the liquor cabinet. He paused, looked across the room at Fabian, and poured himself a tumbler of whiskey. "I see you've got your guitar back." He turned to face his boss.

Fabian's eye's moved to Lucas. He said nothing, just nodded, while his right thumb discreetly flicked the safety back on.

"What happened to your arm?" Lucas asked.

Fabian looked down at his arm, his sleeve was ripped open from cuff to elbow, a deep six-inch gash was slowly leaking blood onto his desk blotter. "No idea. Pour me a whiskey, too."

Lucas poured a second whiskey, carried it over, set it down on the desk, and sat down in one of the leather chairs facing Fabian. "I heard it was a real shit storm down there," Lucas said, before taking a drink of whiskey.

Fabian looked up at Lucas. "It turned into a fucking war." He swallowed about half the whiskey in his glass in one gulp. "I didn't want that, wasn't necessary. If Brennan had just given me the fucking guitar back, we could have worked something out. I knew he was an asshole, but I didn't know he was such a crazy asshole."

Lucas looked up at the polished white guitar which hung on its plaque above Fabian's head. "What's the deal on that guitar anyway. I never took you as a big music fan."

Fabian drank the second half of his whiskey. "Nothing to do with music." He shook his head. "I guess... It's a kind of memorial to my parents."

Lucas took another drink, but said nothing.

"My parents met at Woodstock."

"Woodstock. You mean that big hippy festival in upstate New York."

"That's the one. Three days of music, love and rain." Fabian grinned and held his glass up to show that it was empty.

Lucas stepped over to the liquor cabinet, grabbed the decanter, and poured whiskey into both glasses. He sat back down across from Fabian. "I can't imagine Henry Delbowski hanging around a bunch of hippies in the middle of nowhere upstate New York."

Fabian laughed. "Neither can I. But he was an entrepreneur. My grandparents migrated to the States from Poland when he was three years old. They lived in the tenement housing of Jersey City. My grandfather was a butcher and worked long hours at a meat packing plant. The plant went on strike and he joined the picket lines. On the third day there was some trouble with scabs and the police; my grandfather never came home. The cops told my grandmother, *maybe he ran off.*"

Fabian paused, took a drink, and continued. "My grandmother went to work as a seamstress and commuted to Brooklyn six days a week to work at a sweatshop. My father grew up hustling on the streets of Jersey City. When he heard about the great hippie festival in upstate New York, he knew there was some serious money to be made. He got a loan from a local shark; bought a VW bus, loading it up with kilos of pot, LSD, and whatever else he could get his hands on. He put on a pair of old jeans, tie-dye t-shirt, leather jacket, even wrapped a bandana around his head, and took off for three days of peace, love, music, and hallucinogens."

Lucas, without a word, got up, poured whiskey into both glasses, and sat back down in his chair.

Fabian held up his glass, "Zdrowie." He took a drink, and continued, "He parked his little van right up behind the crowd and set up shop, and just as he'd imagined, business was booming. In fact, business was so good he couldn't weigh out, and sell the bags of marijuana fast enough, and the crowd of customers outside his van was getting bigger and bigger.

Early on the second morning, a beautiful young hippie girl with long wavy auburn hair, asked to buy a dime bag. She saw that he was stressed out, and went to work helping him. In no time, they had a routine. He sat in the back of the van weighing out bags and preparing orders, she was outside doing sales, which worked out a lot better, because she knew the jargon better and was great at dealing with all the hippies looking for a free handout."

"Remi," said Lucas. "Your mother. Unfortunately, I never met her, she was gone by the time I started working for Henry. He talked about her often."

"After mom died, I don't think my old man ever dated again." Fabian set the Desert Eagle on the desk, opened the top left drawer and took out a pack of camels.

"Thought you quit?" asked Lucas.

Fabian ignored the question, lit a cigarette, inhaled deeply, and continued. "On my eighteenth birthday, my old man took me out for a beer. Mom hadn't been gone that long, and he was still in bad shape over losing her. We drank, he asked me about college, but for two hours we mostly sat and drank. And then he told me about Woodstock, and meeting mom, told me the whole story. On the last night of the festival, dad's inventory was sold out, so they went into the van, closed the door and got some much-needed sleep. They awoke early the next morning and made love for the first time, and while making love, far off in the distance, they heard Jimi Hendrix playing the *Star-Spangled Banner*." Fabian put out the cigarette and took a drink of whiskey, "that was when I was conceived."

Lucas said nothing, just stared at his boss, holding a glass of whiskey in his hand.

"He told me my mother wanted to name me Jimi, but obviously she lost that argument because I was named after one of my uncles." Fabian spun around on his seat and looked up at the guitar. "And it was this guitar that Jimi Hendrix played that morning, forty years ago." He spun back around and faced Lucas. "For me, it's a symbol, it tells the story of my parents." Fabian grinned. "My old man would kick my ass for spending so much money on the damned thing."

Lucas smiled, raised his glass, "To Henry and Remi, may they rest in peace."

Fabian raised his glass too, "To my folks."

There was a knock on the door which startled both men, bringing them each out of their own thoughts. A small lean lady with a short bob of black hair and wide lensed glasses stuck her head in the door. "Mr. Delbowski, you have a phone call."

Fabian knew she'd have never bothered him if it weren't important. "Who is it?"

"It's Chicago, sir."

Angry Moon

"Kevin!"

Kevin shot out of the bedroom, a lightning bolt of yellow hair, teeth and tongue, bouncing at Ted's feet. He instinctively knew when Ted would take him for a walk. Ted grabbed the small leather holster with his Glock 19 and clipped it on the back of his belt and pulled his shirt over it. He'd gotten several death threats since the shooting and didn't want to walk around at night without it.

Ted reached down and hooked the leash to Kevin's collar and the two of them made their way down the two flights of stairs to the street. Ted and Kevin had moved into the small one-bedroom apartment two weeks ago, after Sarah had asked him to leave. Ted felt guilty about keeping a big yellow lab in a small one-bedroom unit, but it was all he could find on short notice, the landlord was dog friendly, and it was close to the park.

Kevin was pulling hard on the leash, "What's wrong, boy. You gotta go bad? I just took you out three hours ago." Ted was worried, the way things now, he could take Kevin out six times a day, but when he went back to working eight, ten, or even twelve hours shifts, it wouldn't be fair to leave Kevin alone in the apartment for that many hours. He'd have to find some other arrangement, or worse, find him a new home.

In the park, Ted let out the line another six feet and Kevin ran up to the first tree he came to, gave it a good sniff, then lifted his leg and relieved himself. Kevin was only three years old but had the bladder of an old man. He would never make an eight-hour shift.

The two strolled through the park for fifteen minutes, Ted walking along the path, Kevin hopping through the grass and sniffing every object within reach. They came to a bench in a small clearing, "Let's take a break, boy." It was getting late and had been dark for two hours. He hadn't seen another soul in the park, and although illegal, Ted thought it'd be OK to unleash Kevin. He pulled Kevin in, "Hey!" Once he had the dog's attention he held up his index and middle finger, pointed them at his own eyes, and then at the dog, informing Kevin not to leave his sight.

Kevin hopped around the clearing, doing his sniff and leg routine on every tree and post he came to. Ted took out a cigarette and lit it. He had quit years ago, when he'd gotten into the Police academy, but started again a few weeks ago. He had convinced himself that it was only temporary, to help him cope with all the shit that was going on; getting put on administrative leave, his fiance abandoning him.

Like twenty times a day, Ted's thoughts were drawn back to the night that set his whole life in a tailspin; not even a full month ago. It was a Saturday, September 19th, He and his partner were out on patrol and they'd gotten a 10-70, a prowler, nothing unusual for a Saturday night in Ponopolis. The call came in at 10:37pm about a local car dealership, a place they'd driven by a hundred times on their patrol; Famous Eddy's Cadillacs, a small car dealer on 7th and Baker Street, a dozen new Caddies of various models parked on the front of the lot, another two dozen used trade-ins in the back.

A house across from the dealership had seen someone prowling around the lot, possibly heard glass breaking, and called the police. Ted and his partner were a few blocks away when they got the call. They came in quietly, no lights, no siren.

They pulled directly into the lot and got out of their patrol car. Ted was the senior officer; he signaled his partner to go around the front, he'd go around the back.

He walked along the wall of the showroom to the rear of the lot, holding his standard issue Glock 22 in the two-handed combat grip, his flashlight between his index and middle finger, the syringe technique, just like he had learned at the academy. He was walking along the last row of cars when he heard something; it sounded like someone cursing. He slowly crept around an SUV and saw a man standing next to a car. The suspect had long black hair, but he couldn't make out what he was wearing and couldn't see his face; the man was facing toward the car. There was a lot of broken glass on the ground.

Ted identified himself and told him not to move, the man started turning. The suspect had a dark brown complexion, Ted thought he was Latino. He saw something in his right hand, and yelled, No te muevas! But the suspect kept turning, and then Ted shot him. He didn't remember thinking about it, his finger pulled the trigger and shot the guy. The first time in over ten years on the police force that Ted had fired his weapon. He was aiming for the guy's right shoulder, but the bullet went low and struck him in the chest. The man's body was thrown back up against the car before sliding to the ground.

Ted approached him, looking for his weapon, and found a large pair of scissors still held tightly in his right hand. There was a roll of duct tape on the ground next to him. He heard a flapping sound coming from the car, there was a piece of plastic, a garbage bag half taped to the window frame and it was blowing back and forth in the wind. Ted's partner ran up, and together they administered first aid, but the man died before the ambulance arrived.

He had told this story dozens of times since the shooting. In his report, to his superiors, to Internal Affairs, to his union lawyers, and to his shrink. He had relived it in his mind countless times, until the story grew so numb in his brain, it didn't seem real anymore.

The man he'd shot was Allan Moon, the son of Eddy Moon, the owner of Famous Eddy's Cadillacs. He was closing the place up when he noticed someone had locked the keys of a Chevy Impala in the car. He tried, unsuccessfully, to pop the lock of the car and broke the window in the process. He'd then proceeded to cover the broken window with plastic and duct tape, and that's when Ted and his partner had shown up.

Eddy Moon was a prominent Native American in the area and owned several businesses, including the dealership. The Native American community, the liberals, and the press wanted retribution. An innocent man, just twenty-four years old was dead. Someone's head would roll. Ted had received several death threats.

The worse thing was how people, people Ted had known for years, looked at him now. In some people's eyes Ted saw pity, in other's, he saw a question mark. Was this man, Ted Ryan, a racist?

Ted didn't think of himself as a racist, but over the course of the last four weeks he wasn't sure he even knew what a racist was anymore. Would he have shot the guy if he'd been white? He'd even tried reenacting the event in his mind. But fuck! He thought to himself, more than once, a big part of the blame are the guns. There are over four hundred million guns in America, and most assholes on the street have one. You wait a fraction of a second too long, and you're another statistic—another dead cop.

Ted was still contemplating his dilemma when Kevin barked. "What is it, Kev?"

Kevin made a small hop into the air and barked again. He looked at Ted. He turned back toward the trees; he looked left, then right. He held his nose in the air, catching something on the wind.

"What is it, boy?"

Suddenly, from the right, a small pack of about eight rabbits came rushing out of the bushes, ran along the edge of the clearing before darting between two trees and into the dark.

Ted sat on the bench staring at them as his mind jumped from that night four weeks ago to the present. The last rabbit in the herd who was struggling to keep up, looked more like a guinea pig than a rabbit, Ted thought.

Kevin hesitated, but only for a second, because as soon as the pack disappeared from the clearing, ignoring Ted's previous command to stay in sight, took off after them.

Ted watched Kevin disappear between the trees. He took a moment to massage his temples, looked up, and said, "Shit. Kevin!" He knew hollering wouldn't produce any results. He stood and ran after his dog.

After fighting through a small cluster of woods in the dark, Ted came to another small clearing. There was no sign of Kevin, or the rabbits, but there was a cow eating grass. What the fuck? Ted asked to no one. He heard a bark in the distance and hurried after it.

He worked his way to the right, back to a path where it would be easier going than fighting through bushes and branches. He was jogging along, occasionally hearing a bark, for at least five minutes when he picked up a human voice. He slowed his pace; the voice grew louder. The path looped around a sprawling willow tree. He came into a larger clearing and saw a man standing in the grass and pointing, what looked like a pistol, at a second man who was sitting alone on a park bench. Ted pulled his Glock out and started walking toward the man with the gun. "Police! Don't move!" Ted saw the man turn, and he saw the glint of steel.

The Roadhouse

"Fuck!" The motorcycle's engine puttered to a stop. I looked at the high-tech instrument panel; it had run out of gas. I pulled it to the side of the road and parked it. I looked around, it was about a two-mile walk from here. I assumed Doug was coming after me, but was hoping he didn't know the location of the Roadhouse. I'd wait there for the band.

Five blocks later, Washington Park opened up on the right. It's the largest park in the city; I read once that it's over seven-hundred acres; a mile and a half long and three-quarters of a mile wide.

The Roadhouse is in a run-down warehouse district on the south end of the park. Ktel had come up with its name; a blend from our band name, Road Dust, and the Doors song, *Roadhouse Blues*. It's a twenty-five hundred square foot warehouse built in the late nineteen-forties, a place we had spent many long nights, rehearsing, recording, planning jobs, and sometimes just hanging out drinking beer. A large roll-up door on one end with enough space to park the Winnebago. In the middle section of the building is a kitchen, complete with running water, and the chill-out area: two old sofas, a half-dozen dilapidated chairs, and three beat up tables, a fifty-inch flat-screen TV and an old but adequate sounding stereo. The entire opposite end of the warehouse is our rehearsal area and recording studio, complete with a mixing room—Ktel's headquarters.

I walked to Harriet Street and turned right. The street curved around into the warehouse district, a cluster of relic companies, storage units, and one large ruin that some guy had turned into a skateboard park back in the early nineties.

I used my key and opened the side-door, next to the roll-up door, and went in. It was dark but I could see that the bay where we parked the Dread Sled was empty. I took two steps to the left and felt along the wall for the light-switch.

Wfffrmmm!

Someone, who obviously couldn't play a chord, had strummed on guitar strings. I crouched down and froze next to the wall.

"Go ahead Billy. Turn the lights on."

I knew the voice, and my muscles twinged when I heard it. But what else could I do; I turned the lights on.

Doug was sitting on one of the sofas, he was holding a tired Hohner guitar that Ray used for blues tracks now and again. "You were riding one of the fastest stock bikes on the street, and I still beat you here."

"I ran out of gas."

Doug smiled and then strummed down on the strings again.

"How did you get in here," I asked.

"Please," He paused. "Danny and me were breaking into cabins up in the Northwoods when we were fourteen; It wasn't a challenge."

He wouldn't be here without a gun, I thought. I glanced around, looking for anything to use as a weapon. There was a small table next to the second sofa, but it was a good ten feet away. On the left there were a stack of crates, a broken ride lay on top of them, the cymbal had a crack from the rim halfway to its center.

He tossed the guitar off to the side and stood up. "Dan is right about one thing. I dislike musicians." He shook his head. "They just rub me the wrong way. Know what I mean?"

"Dude, I know exactly what you mean."

He smiled. "I thought you were a loose end. I still do. But now it's personal, you stepped between my brother and me."

Why wait I thought, and I was sick of listening to him. Three steps, it was just three steps to the door. I spun to the left, grabbed the ride cymbal and threw it like a Frisbee at Doug's head. Unfortunately, the crack in it caught the air funny and it sailed off to the right of him; missed him by a good five feet. He laughed as I shot for the door, one step, two steps, three, BAM!

My right side exploded in a fiery pain. The shot blew me through the door. I folded over in pain, my mouth tried to scream, but my lungs didn't have the air.

"Billy, didn't your papa ever tell you, never bring a cymbal to a gunfight." He was getting closer to the door.

As bad as it hurt, I knew, I had to get the fuck away from there. I stumbled back to my feet and made for the corner of the building; every step was excruciating. The animal part of my brain went into fight-or-flight mode. If I could get to the woods behind the warehouse, I could lose him. It was dark and there were a hundred places to hide in the park. I made it behind the building, crossed the drive, and had just reached the tree line.

BAAMM!

The bark of the tree directly in front of me exploded, several wood fragments hit me in the face. I tumbled into the woods; the ground was thick with fall leaves. I must have run a hundred yards before falling into a shallow basin, a depression in the ground about nine feet wide. I was lying on my back, breathing hard, each breath hurt like a bitch. I could feel that my right pant leg was soaked. I carefully unbuttoned my shirt, blood was pumping out of a rough-looking hole about six inches up from my belt line on my right side. I had to stop, or at least slow down the bleeding. I picked up a branch and stuck it between my teeth. I kicked off my Chucks and painfully pulled my socks down using the opposite foot. Lifting my back off the ground an inch was a mother, but I finally got my belt off. I laid the belt on the ground, put one folded sock on it and leaned back, lining up the sock with the entry wound. My head was getting dizzy from the pain, but I had to hurry, I could hear Doug banging through the woods looking for me.

I folded up the second sock and pushed it into the larger exit wound. I couldn't even think of an adjective to describe the pain. It crossed my mind, I'd been wearing these socks for at least three days. I got the belt buckle in place. I had to make it tight enough to hold the socks in place. I pulled the belt tight, buckled it, and then passed out for a minute.

I woke suddenly, something was crashing through the woods, I thought it was Doug; I opened my eyes and saw a pig running faster than I'd have thought pigs could run. It was scraping up leaves with it snout. It snorted at me as it ran by. I wondered briefly why there was a pig in the park. *I gotta get the fuck out of here.*

I rolled over and pushed myself to my feet. I started off to the right again; I knew that side of the park faced a residential area. If I could get to a house?

I tried to keep to the trees, avoid the open areas, but my feet were getting beat up in the woods; I had left my shoes back in the basin. I came to the end of the woods; I hadn't seen or heard Doug, maybe he went the other direction looking for me. There was a large clearing where two paths crossed, two park benches sat at the intersection. I started across the clearing. The sock covering the entry wound on my back must have fallen out, I could feel blood running down into my butt crack. I was losing blood fast, my head felt light, like the blood in my skull was being replaced by air. I walked up to the first park bench; I needed to rest, only for a minute. I sat down.

I looked up at the sky. I tried to steady my breathing. My eyes were heavy, like invisible fingers were pushing down on them, but I knew that if I closed them, I'd pass out, so I forced them open as wide as I could.

"Billy B, have you missed me?" Doug hissed.

I brought my head down. He was walking through the grass towards me; he had a nasty limp which brightened my spirit a little. He stopped about thirty feet in front of me; I could barely make out his features, but I knew he was grinning.

"Go fuck yourself, man." Even talking was exhausting.

He pointed the gun directly at me. "Are you religious Billy?"

"Dude. If you're gonna shoot me, fucking shoot me... I'm tired, and I'm tired of listening to your bullshit. I'd really like to get some sleep."

"Ok Billy." I heard the click of the hammer.

"Police! Don't move!"

Out of nowhere, another guy was standing to the right of Doug.

Doug turned to face him.

"Drop the gun! Now!" said the other dude.

And Doug shot him. The guy folded up in the middle like a flip phone and fell on the ground. Several horrible screams came out of the woods and Doug spun around to look.

Through all this I never moved. I sat on the bench, watched the show, and continued bleeding.

More weird screams came from the woods, but Doug's biggest problem wasn't the woods. The shot-dude wasn't dead. He propped himself up on one arm, aimed his gun and shot Doug. The bullet hit him in the side of the neck. Doug spun back around and fell to his knees. He was facing me now, his eyes wide open. He held his neck where he'd been shot. Blood started oozing out of the side of his mouth.

"That must hurt," I muttered.

The other guy collapsed back to the ground, and Doug, like a tree in the Northwoods, fell flat on his face.

I was gazing at the wild west show in front of me when I heard something to my left. I turned my head and there sat a small yellow monkey on the end of the park bench staring up at me. "Evening." I said.

He stood up on his hind legs, leaned in toward me, sniffed, and let out a high-pierced scream. He then grabbed the top of the bench, flung himself over, and took off across the grass.

"It's a strange night, isn't it?"

I turned my head to the right. There was an old man sitting on the other end of the bench. He wore a ragged shirt, his long black and white hair was held in place with a faded red bandana. His skin was a ruddy leather, like it was carved out of wet clay.

"You couldn't make this shit up on a bad acid trip." I said.

"Life is a funny thing."

"I'd laugh, but it'd hurt too much." I did manage a smile.

"Yes," he turned and looked at me. "You need to go now." He pointed down the path to the right. "Go that way." He smiled. "Now."

"OK." I got up and lurched down the path. I turned around, I had a question, but the old man had already left; there were only two empty park benches.

I came to a hill which led up to the street. It wasn't big, but it was steep. I started up it, about halfway, I fell down. A car drove by on the street twenty feet away. No! I forced myself up, my body felt heavy but empty at the same time. I stumbled up the hill, leaning forward, using my weight for momentum.

I made it to the top and crossed the street, there were no cars in sight. I walked up the front lawn of a house. The lights were on inside. After ringing the front door bell, I fell forward onto the screen door making a bang.

A young guy opened the door and looked at me. "You OK, mister?"

"Nope. Absolutely not." I pushed myself off the door and tried to open it.

"Can I help you?" He asked.

I managed to get the door open and tried to walk into the house, but my foot didn't make the step, and I fell into it.

"Dad!"

A minute later I was looking into an older replica of the last guy's face. "What's your name?" he asked.

"What?" It was an easy question, but my brain felt stuck on it.

"Joey! Call an ambulance." He looked back down at me. "Who are you?" He asked.

I looked up at him, his face was getting all fuzzy. "I'm the bass player." And then I passed out.

The End

Epilogue

Rip: "I got one."

"Let's hear it," said Ktel.

"What do you call a beautiful woman on a bassist's arm?"

Ktel grinned and shrugged. "Tell us."

"A tattoo." Rip slapped his thigh and laughed.

"Yeah, yeah, fuck you guys." I said.

Mal laughed, which made Ktel and Rip laugh, which made me laugh. "Stop it. It still hurts like a fucker to laugh." I almost dropped my wine bottle; almost.

I was lying on the end of a sofa in the Roadhouse propped up on two big pillows that Mal had organized. She'd been fussing over me all afternoon, even tucked a fuzzy blanket around me. I kept looking around the warehouse from Mal, to Ray, Ktel, and Rip. My side still hurt every time I moved, but it didn't matter, it was good to be here, all together again. I couldn't believe the Vegas job was only ten days ago.

Ray was sitting at the dining table which was just off the kitchen, drinking coffee and looking down at a newspaper. "Billy. You seen the headline in the paper?"

"No," I said, "Not sure if I want to."

"*Anarchy in Washington Park*," Ray read.

"Not bad," said Rip, shaking his head.

"That would make an awesome song title," said Ray.

"John Lydon would sue your ass," said Ktel, who was standing over in the rehearsal area splicing some wires together.

"There's enough crazy shit in this article to write a whole album." said Ray, staring down at the paper.

"I'm thrilled I could help whet your creative appetite Ray," I unscrewed the cap from the wine bottle that Rip had gotten me and flicked it ten feet into the garbage can—two points.

"Says here, some unidentified animal rights group broke into a research lab and set all the animals free into the park."

"Where is the place?" asked Mal.

"Over on the west side of the park, not a half mile from here."

"I've lived in Ponopolis my whole life, and I had no idea there was an animal research lab next to the park." I took a good long pull on my bottle. It was chilled to the perfect temperature.

"Not like they advertise," said Ray. "The cop that shot Doug is still in the hospital, but it says he's doing all right; caught a bullet in the hip."

"He was just down the hall from me," I said. "I wheeled down there and thanked him for saving my ass."

"Did you know he was on administrative leave for shooting some Native American dude?"

Ktel looked up from what he was doing. "Fate is a fickle bitch."

"Amen," said Ray.

"Oh, I got another one," said Rip.

"Rip," said Mal, "Leave our wounded bass player alone."

"OK. let's have it, asshole," I said. "But I won't laugh."

"Did you hear the one about the bassist who was so depressed about his timing," Rip smiled, "he jumped behind a train."

Mal started giggling, but put her hand over her mouth, which didn't help because in two seconds everybody was laughing.

"Fuckers! Stop it!" I said, holding my right side, but I didn't care. I felt good. I laughed along with the others, after all, life is a funny thing.

About the Author

Coleman has been a songwriter, and musician, for three decades and has close to sixty published songs. He was Frontman for Blue Manner Haze, Mad Tongues, and several others. Today, he writes and fronts for the band, Sloe Gin. He also teaches and writes for a language institute and German university.

Taking elements from his song lyrics, his time spent with bands; rehearsing, touring, and recording, and together with his love of noir fiction, he has created a unique world of musicians and underworld characters, blending them together in plot twists and humor, in his fictitious city: Ponopolis.

Printed in Poland
by Amazon Fulfillment
Poland Sp. z o.o., Wrocław